Troy stretched out his hand to pull her toward him. She quickly shrank back.

This angered Troy, and he seized her arm and pulled it sharply. Bathsheba gave a quick, low scream.

The scream was followed almost immediately by a deafening explosion. The wall shook, and gray smoke filled the room.

Everyone turned to look at Boldwood. At his back was a gun-rack, as is usual in farmhouses. When Bathsheba had cried out, the veins in Boldwood's face had swollen, and a frenzied look had gleamed in his eye. He had turned quickly, taken one of the guns, and fired it at Troy.

A Background Note about
Far from the Madding Crowd

Far from the Madding Crowd takes place in England in the mid-1800s. At that time, standards of behavior were very different from today's. For instance, people were very aware of the social or economic class to which they belonged, and they associated only with other members of that class. Upper-class folks looked down scornfully on lower-class folks. Lower-class people regarded the upper class with reverence and respect. People in a higher class, especially women, tried to avoid marrying people of a lower economic class. If a woman did make such a choice, people were quick to condemn her for marrying "beneath her class." In *Far from the Madding Crowd*, Bathsheba must choose between marrying the lower-class man she loves and marrying a man she does not love, but who comes from a higher class.

At the time of *Far from the Madding Crowd*, there were also strict rules concerning behavior, rules that seem confining and unfair today. Unmarried women had to wait for a man to make the "first move" in courtship. Unmarried persons were not supposed to kiss each other or even hold hands. There were even "rules" about how a "proper lady" should sit on a horse! Finally, women had few opportunities to earn a living. They could work as housemaids, governesses, nurses, or teachers, but at little else. Thomas Hardy rejected many of these conventions. As a result, many of his heroines engage in behavior that would have been considered shocking at the time his books were published. Look for examples of such behavior in Bathsheba's actions.

Thomas Hardy

Far from the Madding Crowd

Edited by Martin E. Goldstein,
with an Afterword by
Martin E. Goldstein and Janet M. Goldstein

 THE TOWNSEND LIBRARY

FAR FROM THE MADDING CROWD

TP THE TOWNSEND LIBRARY

For more titles in the Townsend Library,
visit our website: www.townsendpress.com

All new material in this edition is
copyright © 2009 by Townsend Press.
Printed in the United States of America

0 9 8 7 6 5 4 3 2 1

Illustrations copyright © 2009 by Hal Taylor

Townsend Press, Inc.
439 Kelley Drive
West Berlin, NJ 08091
cs@townsendpress.com

ISBN-13: 978-1-59194-106-4
ISBN-10: 1-59194-106-7

Library of Congress Control Number:
2007941665

CONTENTS

Afterword

CHAPTER 1

When Farmer Oak smiled, the corners of his mouth spread almost all the way to his ears. His half-closed eyes, with the creases on either side, looked like a drawing of a sunrise.

His first name was Gabriel. He was a young man of sound judgment, proper dress, and general good character. On Sundays, he put on his best clothes and went to church. However, he yawned privately as the service went on. While appearing to be listening intently to the sermon, his thoughts centered upon what there would be for dinner.

On working days, he wore a low-crowned felt hat, jammed tightly upon his head for security in high winds. He wore a long coat, leather pants, and thick boots. These garments were designed more for ruggedness than for style.

Had someone noticed Oak walking across his fields on a certain December morning, he might have noticed that Oak's face was beginning to change in appearance. The shining freshness of youth was giving way to the marks of manhood. He had just reached the time of life when people ceased referring to him as a "young" man. In short, he was twenty-eight and a bachelor.

The field he was in this morning ascended to a ridge called Norcombe Hill. A road connecting two towns ran across this ridge. Casually glancing in this direction, Oak saw, coming down the road toward him, a wagon, painted yellow and gaily decorated. The wagon was drawn by two horses, a wagoner walking alongside. The wagon was loaded with household goods and window plants. On top of this sat a woman, young and attractive. The wagon came to a stop just where Oak was standing behind a tall hedge that concealed him.

"The tailboard of the wagon is gone, Miss," said the wagoner.

"Then I heard it fall," said the girl, in a soft voice. "I heard a noise I could not account for when we were coming up the hill."

"I'll run back."

"Do," she answered.

The girl sat motionless, surrounded by tables and chairs with their legs pointing upwards. There were also pots of geraniums and cactuses, a caged canary, and a cat in a willow basket. The cat surveyed with interest the small birds fluttering around.

After some time, the girl picked up a hand-mirror from her lap and studied her face attentively. She parted her lips and smiled with satisfaction at what she saw. It was a fine morning, and the sun lighted up to a scarlet glow the crimson jacket she wore, and painted a soft luster upon her bright face and dark hair.

Why she should so glance at herself in the middle of the country, instead of in the privacy of her own bedroom, was a puzzle to Farmer Oak. There was no necessity whatever for her looking in the glass. She did not adjust her hat, or pat her hair, or press a dimple into shape. She simply admired herself as a fair product of nature, her thoughts seemingly elsewhere.

The wagoner returned, and she put down the mirror, and the wagon passed on. Before long, the vehicle halted before a tollgate. Oak could overhear a dispute concerning the amount of the toll. The wagoner insistently declared, "The lady says what I've offered ye, you great miser, is enough, and she won't pay any more."

"Very well. Then you can't pass," said the toll-keeper, closing the gate.

Oak looked from one to the other of the parties, who were quarrelling over a mere twopence. "Here," he said, stepping forward and handing two pennies to the gatekeeper. "Let the young woman pass." He looked up at her then. She heard his words, glanced quickly at him, and looked away, then instructed her man to drive on.

The gatekeeper surveyed the retreating vehicle. "That's a handsome maid," he said to Oak.

"But she has her faults," said Gabriel.

"True, Farmer."

"And the greatest of them is—well, what it is always."

"What, then?"

Perhaps Farmer Oak was annoyed by the woman's indifference. He looked back at the spot where she had admired herself in the mirror. "Vanity," Gabriel declared.

CHAPTER 2

It was nearly midnight on the shortest day in the year. A determined wind blew over the hill where Oak had watched the yellow wagon and its occupant in the sunshine of a few days earlier.

The wind sent the dry leaves on the ground rattling against the naked tree trunks with smart taps. Overhead, the sky was remarkably clear. The twinkling of all the stars seemed to be throbs of one body, timed by a common pulse.

Suddenly an unexpected series of sounds began to be heard. They had a clearness which was to be found nowhere in the wind. They were the notes of Farmer Oak's flute.

The tune came from the direction of a small dark object—a shepherd's hut. The hut stood on little wheels, which raised its floor about a foot from the ground. Such shepherds' huts are dragged into the fields at that time of year when lambs give birth, to shelter the shepherd in his enforced nightly attendance.

It was only recently that people had begun to call Gabriel "Farmer" Oak. During the twelve months preceding this time, he had been enabled by hard work and good spirits to lease the small sheep-farm where he presently lived. He had also managed to

5

stock the farm with two hundred sheep. Previously he had been a bailiff, or general manager of another's farm. Earlier still, he had been only a shepherd. He had helped tend sheep from childhood on.

This venture into the paths of farming as master, not hired hand, was a critical time for Gabriel Oak. The risk was all the higher, since he had yet to pay for the sheep. He counted on the wool of these animals to pay off the loan he had taken out to buy them. The increase of his flock at the present birthing season would be a large help to his financial situation.

Oak went out of the hut to his nearby flock. He returned to the hut, bringing in his arms a newborn lamb. The little speck of life he placed on a wisp of hay before the small stove, where a can of milk was simmering. Oak extinguished the lantern by blowing into it. He lay down on a rather hard couch, formed of a few corn sacks thrown carelessly down. In no time Farmer Oak was asleep.

The inside of the hut was cozy and comfortable. A fire cast a warm glow over the stock of bread, bacon, cheese, and a cup for ale or cider. Beside these provisions lay the flute. The house was ventilated by two round holes with wood slides.

The lamb, revived by the warmth, began to bleat. The sound entered Gabriel's ears and brought him to full wakefulness. He put on his hat, took the lamb in his arms, and carried it into the darkness. After placing the little creature with its mother, he stood and carefully examined the sky, to figure out the time of night from the altitudes of the stars.

"One o'clock," said Gabriel.

As he looked into the distance, Oak gradually perceived that what he had previously taken to be a low star was in reality no such thing. It was an artificial light, almost close at hand.

Now, the land that made up Oak's farm was ground he had leased from a sizeable farm, which contained many acres besides those tended by Oak. The light Oak spied came from the direction of the large farm adjoining his own.

Farmer Oak went toward the light, which came from a primitive shed. The structure was formed of boards nailed to posts and covered with tar as a preservative. Oak approached the shed and peered in through a hole.

The place contained two women and two cows. By the side of the latter a steaming bran-mash stood in a bucket. One of the women was past middle age. Her companion was apparently young and graceful. Oak could not see her clearly, as she had wrapped herself in a large cloak.

"There, now we'll go home," said the elder of the two, resting her knuckles upon her hips. "I do hope Daisy will get better now. I have never been more frightened in my life, but I don't mind breaking my rest if she recovers."

The young woman yawned but managed to say, "I wish we were rich enough to pay a man to do these things."

"As we are not, we must do them ourselves," said the other. "You must help me if you stay."

"Well, my hat is gone," continued the younger.

"The wind must have blown it off my head."

The cow standing erect was of the Devon breed, as uniformly dark red as if the animal had been dipped in a dye of that color. The other was spotted, gray and white. Beside her Oak now noticed a little calf about a day old, looking idiotically at the two women.

"I think we had better send for some oatmeal," said the elder woman. "There's no more bran."

"Yes, Aunt. I'll ride over for it as soon as it is light."

"But there's no sidesaddle."

"I can ride on the regular kind of saddle. Trust me."

Oak, upon hearing these remarks, became more curious to observe the younger woman's face. In a happy coincidence, the girl now dropped the cloak, and out tumbled curls of black hair over a red jacket. Oak knew her instantly as the heroine of the yellow wagon and lookingglass, also as the woman who owed him twopence.

The women placed the calf beside its mother again, took up the lantern, and went out to the main house. Gabriel Oak returned to his flock.

CHAPTER 3

The sluggish day began to break. For no particular reason except that the incident of the night had occurred there, Oak walked again toward the big house. When he stopped, he heard the steps of a horse at the foot of the hill. Soon he could see an auburn pony with a girl on its back, ascending by the path leading past the cattle shed. She was the young woman of the night before. Gabriel instantly thought of the hat she had mentioned as having gotten lost in the wind. Possibly she had come to look for it. He hastily looked about. After walking about ten yards, he found the hat among the leaves. Gabriel took it in his hand and returned to his hut. Here he remained and peeped through the vent hole in the direction of the rider's approach.

She came up and looked around. Gabriel was about to advance and restore the missing article when an unexpected spectacle persuaded him to hold off. The path followed by the horse was not a bridle path. It was no more than a walking trail. Tree branches spread horizontally at a height not greater than seven feet above the ground, which made it impossible to ride erect beneath them. The girl, who wore no riding-habit, looked around for a moment, as if to assure herself that no one could see her. Then she gracefully dropped backward, flat upon the pony's back, her head over its tail, her feet against its shoulders, and her eyes to the sky. She glided into this position as rapidly as a kingfisher and as silently as a hawk. Gabriel's eyes had scarcely been able to follow her. The tall lank pony seemed used to such doings, and ambled along unconcerned. Thus she passed under the level boughs, riding in an extremely unladylike manner.

Once past the trail, she sat up straight and again peered around to make sure no one was in sight. Satisfying herself on that score, she seated herself in the manner demanded by the saddle, which was not designed for riding side-saddle, as a woman was expected to ride. Seated in this immodest position, she trotted off in the direction of Tewnell Mill.

Oak was amused, even a little astonished, at the girl's daring behavior. Hanging up the hat in his hut, he went again among his flock. An hour passed, and the girl returned, properly seated now, with a bag of bran in front of her. On nearing the cattle-shed, she was met by a boy bringing a milking-pail, who held the reins of the pony while she slid off. The boy led away the horse, leaving the pail with the young woman.

Soon soft spurts alternating with loud spurts came in regular succession from within the shed, the obvious sounds of a person milking a cow. Gabriel took the lost hat in his hand and waited beside the path she would follow in leaving the shed.

She came, the pail in her right hand, while she extended her left arm as a balance. Her face and figure were classically beautiful. Enough of her arm was bare to make Oak wish that the event had happened in the summer, when her entire arm would have been revealed. It was with some surprise, but no embarrassment, that she saw Gabriel's face rising like the moon behind the hedge. In fact, Gabriel was the one who blushed.

"I found a hat," said Oak.

"It is mine," said she, trying not to laugh. "It flew away last night."

"One o'clock this morning?"

"Well—it was." She was surprised. "How did you know?" she said.

"I was here."

"You are Farmer Oak, are you not?"

"Yes. I'm lately come to this place."

"Have you a large farm?" she inquired, looking around, and swinging back her black hair.

"No; not large. About a hundred acres."

"I wanted my hat this morning," she went on. "I had to ride to Tewnell Mill."

"Yes, you did."

"How do you know?"

"I saw you."

"Where?" she inquired in a tone of great anxiety.

"Here—going through the fields and down the hill," said Farmer Oak.

At this remark, the girl's face reddened with embarrassment, as she recalled her unladylike antics on the horse. Oak withdrew his own eyes from hers as suddenly as if he had been caught in a theft.

When he looked in her direction again, the girl had slipped away.

Five mornings and evenings passed. The young woman came regularly to milk the healthy cow or to attend to the sick one, but never allowed her vision to stray in the direction of Oak's person. His lack of tact had deeply offended her—not by seeing what he could not help, but by letting her know that he had seen it.

The acquaintanceship might have ended in a slow forgetting, but for an incident which occurred at the end of the same week. One afternoon it began to freeze. It was a time when in cottages the breath of the sleepers freezes to the sheets; when round the drawing-room fire of a thick-walled mansion the sitters' backs are cold, even while their faces are all aglow. Many a small bird went to bed supperless that night among the bare boughs.

As the milking-hour drew near, Oak kept his usual watch upon the cowshed. At last he felt cold. After placing an extra quantity of bedding around the newborn lambs, he entered the hut and heaped more fuel upon the stove. The wind came in at the bottom of the door, and to prevent it, Oak laid a sack there and wheeled the cot round a little more to the south. Then the wind spouted in at a ventilating hole—of which there was one on each side of the hut.

Gabriel had always known that when the fire was lighted and the door closed, one of these must be kept open—the one on the side away from the wind. Closing the slide to windward, he turned to open the other. On second thought, the farmer considered that he would first sit down leaving both closed for a minute or two, till the temperature of the hut was a little raised. He sat down. Weariness overcame him, and he fell asleep.

How long he remained so Gabriel never knew. During the first stages of his return to wakefulness, he sensed that something peculiar was happening. His dog was howling, his head was aching fearfully, and someone's hands were loosening his neckerchief.

On opening his eyes, he found that the young girl who had lost her hat was beside him. To his astonishment, his head was upon her lap, his face and neck were disagreeably wet, and her fingers were unbuttoning his collar.

"Whatever is the matter?" said Oak, vacantly.

She seemed to suppress a little smile.

"Nothing now," she answered, "since you are not dead. It is a wonder you were not suffocated in this hut of yours."

"Ah, the hut!" murmured Gabriel. "I gave ten pounds for that hut. But I'll sell it, and sit under thatched hurdles as they did in old times, and curl up to sleep in a lock of straw! It played me nearly the same trick the other day!" Gabriel, by way of emphasis, brought down his fist upon the floor.

"It was not exactly the fault of the hut," she observed. "You should not have been so foolish as to leave the slides closed."

"Yes, I suppose you're right," said Oak, absently. He was trying to capture and appreciate the sensation of being with her, his head upon her lap, before the event passed on into the heap of bygone things. He wished she knew his feelings for her. But not being skilled with language, he remained silent.

She made him sit up, and then Oak began wiping his face and shaking himself. "How can I thank 'ee?" he said at last, gratefully, some of the natural rusty red having returned to his face.

"Oh, never mind that," said the girl, smiling.

"How did you find me?"

"I heard your dog howling and scratching at the door of the hut when I came to the milking shed. You were lucky. Daisy's milking is almost over for the season, and I shall not come here after this week or the next. The dog saw me, and jumped over to me, and laid hold of my skirt. I came across and looked round the hut to see if the slides were closed. My uncle has a hut like this one, and I have heard him tell his shepherd not to go to sleep without leaving a slide open. I opened the door, and there you were, like dead. I threw the milk over you, as there was no water, forgetting it was warm, and no use."

"I wonder if I should have died?" Gabriel said.

"Oh no!" the girl replied. She seemed to prefer a less tragic probability. To have saved a man from death would have made the neighbors gossip.

"I believe you saved my life, Miss—I don't know your name. I know your aunt's, but not yours."

"I would just as soon not tell it. There is no reason why I should, as you probably will never have much to do with me."

"Still, I should like to know."

"You can inquire at my aunt's—she will tell you."

"My name is Gabriel Oak."

"And mine isn't. You seem fond of yours in speaking it so decisively, Gabriel Oak."

"You see, it is the only one I shall ever have, and I must make the most of it."

"I always think mine sounds odd and disagreeable."

"I should think you might soon get a new one."

"Mercy!—how many opinions you express concerning other people, Gabriel Oak."

"Well, Miss—excuse the words—I thought you would like them. But I can't match you, I know, in expressing my thoughts in words. I never was very clever. But I thank you. Come, give me your hand."

She hesitated for a moment. "Very well," she said, and gave him her hand. He held it only for an instant. In his fear of showing too much devotion, Oak swerved to the opposite extreme, touching her fingers with the lightness of a person who lacked any feelings.

"I am sorry," he said the instant after.

"What for?"

"Letting your hand go so quickly."

"You may have it again if you like; there it is." She gave him her hand again.

Oak held it longer this time—indeed, curiously long. "How soft it is—being wintertime, too—not chapped or rough or anything!" he said.

"There—that's long enough," said she, though without pulling it away. "But I suppose you are thinking you would like to kiss it? You may if you want to."

"I wasn't thinking of any such thing," said Gabriel, simply; "but I will—"

"Then you won't!" She snatched back her hand. Gabriel knew he had said the wrong thing.

"Now find out my name," she said, teasingly, and withdrew.

CHAPTER 4

Oak was so enchanted by this young girl that he continued to watch through the hedge in the hope of gaining a glimpse of her on the way to milking. The longer he watched for her, the stronger his feelings grew. By making inquiries, he found that the girl's name was Bathsheba Everdene, and that the cow would go dry in about seven days. He dreaded the eighth day.

At last the eighth day came. The cow had ceased to give milk for that year, and Bathsheba came up the hill no more. Gabriel had reached a pitch of existence he never could have anticipated a short time before. He liked saying "Bathsheba" instead of whistling. He now favored black hair, though he had sworn by brown ever since he was a boy. Oak even found himself vowing, to himself, "I'll make her my wife, or upon my soul I shall be good for nothing!"

All this while he was trying to figure out an excuse that would allow him to visit the cottage of Bathsheba's aunt.

He found his opportunity in the death of a ewe, the mother of a living lamb. On a fine January morning, Oak put the lamb into a respectable Sunday basket, and he stalked across the fields to the house of Mrs. Hurst, the aunt. George, Oak's dog, trailed behind, looking greatly concerned at the serious turn country affairs seemed to be taking.

In preparation for this visit, Oak dressed himself between the carefully neat and the carelessly elegant. He thoroughly cleaned his silver watch-chain, put new lacing straps on his boots, selected a new walkingstick, took a new handkerchief from the bottom of his clothesbox, put on the light waistcoat patterned all over with sprigs of roses and lilies, and used all the hair oil he possessed upon his usually dry, sandy, and curly hair.

Just as Oak arrived by the garden gate, he saw a cat inside, going into various arched shapes and fiendish convulsions at the sight of his dog George. The dog took no notice, for he had arrived at an age at which he regarded unnecessary barking as a waste of breath.

A voice came from behind some laurel-bushes into which the cat had run: "Poor dear! Did a nasty brute of a dog want to kill it;—did he, poor dear!"

"I beg your pardon," said Oak to the voice, "but George was walking on behind me with a temper as mild as milk."

Nobody answered, and he heard the person retreat among the bushes.

Oak went up to the door and knocked. Bathsheba's aunt appeared.

"Will you tell Miss Everdene that somebody would be glad to speak to her?" said Mr. Oak.

Bathsheba was out. The voice had evidently been hers.

"Will you come in, Mr. Oak?"

"Oh, thank 'ee," said Gabriel, following her to the fireplace. "I've brought a lamb for Miss Everdene. I thought she might like one to raise; girls do."

"She might," said Mrs. Hurst, musingly; "though she's only a visitor here. If you will wait a minute, Bathsheba will be in."

"Yes, I will wait," said Gabriel, sitting down. "The lamb isn't really the business I came about, Mrs. Hurst. In short, I was going to ask her if she'd like to be married."

"And were you indeed?"

"Yes. Because if she would, I should be very glad to marry her. D'ye know if she's got any other young man hanging about her at all?"

"Let me think," said Mrs. Hurst, poking the fire. "Yes—bless you, ever so many young men. You see, Farmer Oak, she's so good-looking, and very bright besides—she was going to be a governess once, you know, only she was too wild. Not that her young men ever come here—but, Lord, in the nature of women, she must have a dozen!"

"That's unfortunate," said Farmer Oak, staring at a crack in the stone floor with sorrow. "I'm only an everyday sort of man, and my only chance was in being the first to offer. Well, there's no use in my waiting, for that was all I came about. So, I'll take myself home, Mrs. Hurst."

When Gabriel had gone about two hundred yards, he heard someone calling to him. He looked round and saw a girl racing after him, waving a white handkerchief.

Oak stood still, and the runner drew nearer. It was Bathsheba Everdene. "Farmer Oak—I—" she said, pausing for lack of breath and putting her hand to her side.

"I have just called to see you," said Gabriel.

"Yes, I know that," she said panting like a robin, her face red and moist from her exertions, like a peony petal before the sun dries off the dew. "I didn't know you had come to ask to marry me, or I should have come in from the garden instantly. I ran after you to say that my aunt made a mistake in sending you away from courting me—"

Gabriel's heart swelled. "I'm sorry to have made you run so fast, my dear," he said. "Wait a bit till you've found your breath."

"It was quite a mistake—my aunt's telling you I had a young man already," Bathsheba went on. "I haven't a sweetheart at all—and I never had one."

"Really and truly I am glad to hear that!" said Farmer Oak, smiling one of his long, special smiles, and blushing with gladness. He held out his hand to take hers. As soon as he seized it, she put it behind her, so that it slipped through his fingers like an eel.

"I have a nice snug little farm," said Gabriel, with a little less assurance than when he had seized her hand. "A man has advanced me money to begin with, but it will soon be paid off. And though I am only an everyday sort of man, I have got on a little since I was a boy." He continued: "When we are married, I am quite sure I can work twice as hard as I do now."

"Why, Farmer Oak," she said, "I never said I was going to marry you."

"Well—that IS a tale!" said Oak, with dismay. "To run after anybody like this, and then say you don't want him!"

"What I meant to tell you was only this, that nobody has got me yet as a sweetheart, instead of my having a dozen, as my aunt said. I *hate* to be thought men's property in that way, though possibly I shall be some day. Why, if I'd wanted you, I shouldn't have run after you like this; it would have been much too forward! But there was no harm in hurrying to correct a piece of false news that had been told you."

"Oh, no—no harm at all. Well, I am not quite certain it was no harm."

"Indeed, I hadn't time to think whether I wanted to marry or not."

"Come," said Gabriel, brightening again. "Think a minute or two. I'll wait a while, Miss Everdene. Will you marry me? Do, Bathsheba. I love you far more than common!"

"I'll try to think," she said.

"But you can give a guess."

"Then give me time." Bathsheba looked thoughtfully into the distance, away from the direction in which Gabriel stood.

"I can make you happy," he said to the back of her head. "You shall have a piano in a year or two—farmers' wives are getting to have pianos now—and I'll practice the flute right well to play with you in the evenings."

"Yes; I should like that."

"And have nice flowers, and birds—roosters and hens I mean, because they are useful," continued Gabriel, feeling balanced between poetry and practicality.

"I should like it very much."

"And a frame for cucumbers—like a gentleman and lady."

"Yes."

"And when the wedding was over, we'd have it put in the newspaper list of marriages."

"Dearly I should like that!"

"And the babies in the births—every one of 'em! And at home by the fire, whenever you look up, there I shall be—and whenever I look up, there you will be."

"Wait, wait, and don't be improper!"

Her face became serious, and she was silent a while. Then she decisively turned to him. "No; 'tis no use," she said. "I don't want to marry you."

"Try."

"I have tried hard all the time I've been thinking. A marriage would be very nice in one sense. People would talk about me, and think I had won my battle, and I should feel triumphant, and all that. But a husband—"

"Well!"

"Why, he'd always be there, as you say. Whenever I looked up, there he'd be."

"Of course he would—I, that is."

"Well, what I mean is that I shouldn't mind being a bride at a wedding, if I could be one without having a husband. But since a woman can't show off in that way by herself, I shan't marry—at least yet."

"Upon my heart and soul, I don't know what a maid can say stupider than that," said Oak. "But, dearest," he continued, "why won't you have me?"

"I cannot," she said, retreating.

"But why?" he persisted, standing still at last in despair of ever reaching her.

"Because I don't love you."

"But I love you—and, as for myself, I am content to be liked."

"Oh, Mr. Oak—that's very fine! You'd get to despise me."

"Never," said Mr. Oak. "I shall do one thing in this life—one thing certain—that is, love you, and long for you, and keep wanting you till I die."

"It seems dreadfully wrong not to accept you when you feel so much!" she said with a little distress. "How I wish I hadn't run after you! I want somebody to tame me. I am too independent, and you would never be able to, I know."

Oak cast his eyes across the field in a way that suggested it was useless to argue.

"Mr. Oak," she said, "you are better off than I. I have hardly a penny in the world. I am staying with my aunt for my bare sustenance. I am better educated than you, and I don't love you a bit. That's my side of the case. Here's yours: you are a farmer just beginning. If you marry at all (which you should certainly not think of doing at present), you should marry a woman with money. She would stock a larger farm for you than you have now."

Gabriel looked at her with a little surprise and much admiration. "That's the very thing I had been thinking myself!" he naively said.

Bathsheba was not pleased at all by these words. "Well, then, why did you come and disturb me?" she said almost angrily, an enlarging red spot rising in each cheek.

"I can't do what I think would be—would be—"

"Right?"

"No, wise."

"After what you have just said, Mr. Oak, do you think I could marry you? Certainly not."

He broke in passionately. "Because I am honest enough to say what every man in my shoes would have thought of, you are angry with me. That talk about your not being good enough for me is nonsense. You talk like a well-bred lady; everyone in the parish notices it. And your uncle at Weatherbury is, I have heard, a large farmer—much larger than ever I shall be. May I call in the evening, or will you walk along with me on Sundays? I don't want you to make up your mind at once, if you'd rather not."

"No—no—I cannot do those things with you. Don't press me any more—don't. I don't love you— so 'twould be ridiculous," she said, with a laugh.

"Very well," said Oak, with an air of utter resignation. "Then I'll ask you no more."

Chapter 5

Not long after, news reached Gabriel that Bathsheba Everdene had left the area and gone to a place called Weatherbury, more than twenty miles away. However, Oak was unable to discover whether she journeyed there as a temporary visitor, as a permanent resident, or in some other capacity.

Gabriel had two dogs. George, the elder, had an ebony-tipped nose and a reddish brown coat. Though old, he was clever and trustworthy still.

The younger dog, George's son, would take over when George died. The younger dog was just learning his trade. If he had a fault, it was that he had difficulty in distinguishing between doing a thing well enough and doing it too well. Thus, if sent behind the flock to move them forward, he did it so thoroughly that he would have chased them across the whole county if not called off.

On the further side of Norcombe Hill was a chalk-pit, from which chalk had been drawn for generations. Two hedges converged upon it in the form of a V, but without quite meeting. The narrow opening left, which was immediately over the rim of the deep pit, was protected by a semi-decayed railing.

One night, when Farmer Oak had returned to his house, he called as usual to the dogs for them to come in. Only one responded—old George. The other could not be found, either in the house, lane, or garden. Gabriel then remembered that he had left the two dogs on the hill eating a dead lamb. Concluding that the young one had not finished his meal, he went indoors and went to bed.

It was a still, moist night. Just before dawn he was assisted in waking by an unusual sound coming from the flock. Usually, the bells on the animals tinkled in an irregular and idle manner, indicating all was well. This particular morning the bells were sounding with unusual violence and rapidity. Oak's experienced ear told him the flock was running at breakneck speed.

He jumped out of bed, dressed, tore down the lane through a foggy dawn, and ascended the hill. When he arrived at the grazing ground, he was astonished to find hardly any of his two hundred sheep wandering about. They seemed to have vanished. Then he saw the younger dog standing at the edge of the chalk pit, silhouetted against the sky.

A horrible thought darted through Oak as he raced to the edge of the chalk pit. The barrier protecting the rim was broken through. At the bottom of the chalk pit he spied the flock, lying dead and mangled. The younger dog came up, licked his hand, and made signs implying that he expected some great reward for doing such a thorough job.

Oak was an intensely humane man. His first feeling was one of pity for the untimely death of these gentle creatures.

It took a second to remember another phase of the matter. The sheep were not insured. His entire life savings were gone. His hopes of being an independent farmer were laid low—possibly forever. He leaned down upon a rail and covered his face with his hands.

Recovering at last, the one sentence he uttered was in thankfulness: "Thank God I am not married. What would SHE have done in the poverty now coming upon me!"

It appeared that the poor young dog had learned his lessons too well. He was kept for running after sheep. He therefore assumed that the more he ran after them, the better. And so, energized by his late meal, he had chased the sheep clear over the edge of the chalk pit, to their deaths.

George's son had done his work so thoroughly that he was considered too good a workman to live. Gabriel shot him that same day.

Gabriel's farm had been stocked by a dealer who was receiving a percentage from the farmer till such time as the advance should be paid off. Oak found that the value of all his possessions would be about sufficient to pay his debts. That left him a free man with the clothes he stood up in, and nothing more.

Chapter 6

Two months passed. We come to a day in February, on which was held the yearly hiring fair in the town of Casterbridge.

At one end of the street stood from two to three hundred workers hoping to get hired for the summer season. These included carters and wagoners, thatchers, shepherds, and some others.

In the crowd was an athletic young fellow of somewhat superior appearance to the rest. This was Gabriel Oak, who was looking for a position as a bailiff, or manager, of a farming property.

Gabriel was paler now. His eyes were more thoughtful, and his expression was more sad. He had passed through a wretched ordeal that had left him indifferent to his fate. Thus, he achieved a dignified calm he had never before known.

This state of mind enabled him to accept the absence of any offers for his services. He did learn that another hiring fair was to be held in the town of Shottsford the next day.

"How far is Shottsford?" Oak inquired.

"Ten miles t'other side of Weatherbury."

Weatherbury! It was where Bathsheba had gone two months before. Oak's heart lit up.

"How far is it to Weatherbury?"

"Five or six miles."

Bathsheba had probably left Weatherbury long before this time. However, Oak decided to go to the Shottsford fair because it lay near Weatherbury. Oak resolved to sleep at Weatherbury that night on his way to Shottsford.

As his weary feet neared Weatherbury, he noticed an unusual light about half a mile distant. Oak watched it, and the glow increased. Something was on fire.

Oak ran in the direction of the flames. The fire was beginning to consume a farm's entire crop of wheat for the year, a financial disaster about to happen. Racing toward the flames, Gabriel saw that he was not alone. People were calling out. "Oh, Mark Clark—come! And you, Billy Smallbury—and you, Maryann Money—and you, Jan Coggan, and Matthew there!" The group of men set to work with a remarkable confusion of purpose.

Oak knew exactly what to do and began shouting orders. "Stop the draft under the wheat-rick! Get a tarpaulin—quick!"

These measures helped contain the fire. But now the flames threatened the huge roof covering the wheat-stacks. Oak scrambled up to the top of one of the stacks, grabbed some sheaths of wheat, and beat back the flames that had started to burn the roof.

At some distance from the intense heat stood a pony, bearing a young woman on its back. To protect her face from the heat, she wore a dark veil. By her side was another woman, on foot.

"He's a shepherd," said the woman on foot. "And his coat is burnt in two holes, I declare! A fine young shepherd he is too, Ma'am."

"Whose shepherd is he?" said the woman on the pony, in a clear voice.

"Don't know, Ma'am."

"Don't any of the others know?"

"Nobody at all—I've asked 'em. Quite a stranger, they say."

The young woman on the pony rode forward and looked anxiously around. "Do you think the barn is safe?" she said.

"D'ye think the barn is safe, Jan Coggan?" said the second woman, passing on the question to the nearest man in that direction.

"Safe—now—leastwise I think so. If this rick had caught fire, the barn would have followed. 'Tis that bold shepherd up there that has done the most to contain the fire."

"He does work hard," said the young woman on horseback, looking up at Gabriel through her thick wool coat. "I wish he was shepherd here. Don't any of you know his name?"

"Never heard the man's name in my life, or seen him afore."

The fire began to die down. Gabriel climbed down the ladder.

"Maryann," said the girl on horseback, "go to him and say that the farmer wishes to thank him for the great service he has done."

Maryann stalked off toward the rick and met Oak at the foot of the ladder. She delivered her message.

"Where is your master the farmer?" asked Gabriel, hopeful that he might gain employment.

"'Tisn't a master; 'tis a mistress, shepherd."

"A woman farmer?"

"Ay, and a rich one too!" said a bystander. "Lately she came here from a distance. Took on her uncle's farm, who died suddenly. Had lots of money."

"That's she, back there upon the pony," said Maryann.

Oak, his face smudged and grimy, his coat burnt into holes and dripping with water, advanced toward the woman in the saddle. He lifted his hat with respect and said in a hesitating voice, "Do you happen to want a shepherd, Ma'am?"

She lifted the veil tied round her face, and looked astonished. Gabriel and his cold-hearted darling, Bathsheba Everdene, were face to face.

Bathsheba did not speak, and he mechanically repeated, "Do you want a shepherd, Ma'am?"

CHAPTER 7

Bathsheba sensed the awkwardness of the situation. Yet she was not embarrassed, even as she remembered Gabriel's declaration of love to her at Norcombe.

"Yes," she murmured, putting on an air of dignity, and turning again to him. "I do want a shepherd. But—"

"He's the very man, Ma'am," said one of the villagers, quietly.

"Ay, that he is," said a second.

"The man, truly!" said a third, with heartiness.

"Then will you tell him to speak to the bailiff," said Bathsheba.

The bailiff was pointed out to Gabriel. The two men retired to talk over the necessary preliminaries of hiring.

Bathsheba then rode off, and the men straggled on to the village in twos and threes.

"And now," said the bailiff, finally, "all is settled, I think, about your coming, and I am going home. Goodnight to ye, shepherd."

"Can you get me a lodging?" inquired Gabriel.

"That I can't, indeed," he said. "If you follow on the road till you come to Warren's Malthouse, where they are all gone to have a bite to eat, I daresay some of 'em will tell you of a place. Goodnight to ye, shepherd."

Oak walked on to the village, still astonished at the meeting with Bathsheba. He was glad to be near her. He was also surprised at how quickly the inexperienced girl of Norcombe had developed into the cool, supervising woman here. But some women require only an emergency to make them fit for one.

Oak directed his steps in the direction of the Malthouse. Passing through the churchyard, he noticed a figure standing by a tree. It was a slim girl, dressed in poor-looking clothes.

"Goodnight to you," said Gabriel, heartily.

"Goodnight," said the girl to Gabriel.

"I'll thank you to tell me if I'm headed toward Warren's Malthouse?" Gabriel resumed.

"Quite right. It's at the bottom of the hill. And do you know—" The girl hesitated and then went on again. "Do you know how late they keep open the Buck's Head Inn?"

"I don't know where the Buck's Head is, or anything about it. Do you think of going there tonight?"

"Yes—" The woman again paused. "You are not a Weatherbury man?" she said, timidly.

"I am not. I am the new shepherd—just arrived."

"You won't say anything in the parish about having seen me here, will you—at least, not for a day or two?"

"I won't if you wish me not to," said Oak.

"Thank you, indeed," the other replied. "I am rather poor, and I don't want people to know anything about me." Then she was silent and shivered.

"You ought to have a cloak on such a cold night," Gabriel observed. "Since you are not very well off, perhaps you would accept this trifle from me. It is only a shilling, but it is all I have to spare."

"Yes, I will take it," said the stranger gratefully.

She extended her hand; Gabriel did the same. In feeling for each other's palm in the gloom before the money could be passed, a tiny incident occurred which told much. Gabriel's fingers alighted on the young woman's wrist. It was beating with a throb of tragic intensity. He had frequently felt the same quick, hard heartbeat in his lambs when they had been overdriven. It suggested that her vital forces— already, to judge from her figure and stature, very low—were quickly being consumed.

"What is the matter?"

"Nothing."

"But there is?"

"No, no, no! Let your having seen me be a secret!"

"Very well; I will. Goodnight, again."

"Goodnight."

The young girl remained motionless by the tree, and Gabriel descended into the village of Weatherbury. He sensed that he had been in the presence of a very deep sadness when touching that slight and fragile creature.

CHAPTER 8

Warren's Malthouse was surrounded by an old wall covered with ivy. From the walls an overhanging thatched roof sloped up to a point in the center. Through a single glass pane in the front door, red comfortable rays now stretched out upon the ivied wall in front. Voices could be heard inside.

Oak's hand skimmed the surface of the door till he found a leather strap, which he pulled. This lifted a wooden latch, and the door swung open.

The room inside was lighted only by the ruddy glow from the fireplace. The stone floor was worn into a path from the doorway to the fireplace. In a remote corner was a small bed, where the maltster who owned the establishment slept.

This aged man was now sitting opposite the fire, his frosty white hair and beard overgrowing his gnarled figure like gray moss and lichen upon a leafless apple tree.

Gabriel's nose was greeted by the sweet smell of new malt. The conversation (which seemed to have concerned the origin of the fire) immediately ceased. The patrons eyed the new arrival carefully. Several exclaimed,

"Oh, 'tis the new shepherd, 'a b'lieve."

"We thought we heard a hand pawing about

the door," said one. "Come in, shepherd. Ye be welcome, though we don't know yer name."

"Gabriel Oak, that's my name, neighbors."

The ancient maltster turned around at this.

"That's never Gable Oak's grandson over at Norcombe—never!" he said.

"My father and my grandfather were old men of the name of Gabriel," said the shepherd.

"Thought I knowed the man's face as I seed him at the fire! And where be ye goin' now, shepherd?"

"I'm thinking of staying here," said Mr. Oak.

"Knowed yer grandfather for years and years!" continued the maltster. "Knowed yer grandmother. Yer father too. My grandson William must have knowed the very man afore us—didn't ye, Billy, afore ye left Norcombe?"

"Aye," said Billy. "The other day I and my youngest daughter, Liddy, were over at my grandson's christening," continued Billy. "We were talking about this very family."

"Come, shepherd, and drink," proclaimed the maltster. Taking the two-handled tall mug, he drank a hearty amount and passed it to the next man. This was a brisk young man—Mark Clark by name. He was a friendly and pleasant individual, who was quite fond of drink, and who usually managed to get someone else to pay for his liquid refreshment.

"And here's a mouthful of bread and bacon that mis'ess have sent, shepherd. The cider will go down better with a bit of victuals. Don't ye chew too carefully, shepherd, for I let the bacon fall in the road outside as I was bringing it in, and may be 'tis rather gritty. But, 'tis clean dirt."

"Drink up, Henry Fray—drink," said Jan Coggan insistently.

Henry did not hesitate. He was a man of more than middle age, with eyebrows high up in his forehead. He always signed his name "Henery"—strenuously insisting upon that spelling.

Mr. Jan Coggan, who had passed the cup to Henry, was a red-faced man with a mirthful glimmer in his eye. His name often appeared on the marriage register of Weatherbury and neighboring parishes as best man and chief witness in countless unions of the previous twenty years.

"Why, Joseph Poorgrass, ye han't had a drop!" said Mr. Coggan to a self-conscious man in the background, thrusting the cup they all drank from toward him. Poorgrass's most notable trait was a painful shyness.

Gabriel then inquired, "What sort of a place is this to live at, and what sort of a mis'ess is she to work for?" Gabriel's chest swelled as he gave voice to the innermost subject of his heart.

"We know little of her," said one. "She only showed herself a few days ago. Her uncle just died. As I take it, she's going to run the farm."

"'Tis a very good family," said Jan Coggan. "Her uncle was a very fair sort of man."

"And did any of you know Miss Everdene's father and mother?" inquired the shepherd.

"I knew them a little," said the maltster's son,

Jacob Smallbury, about sixty-five years old. "But they were townsfolk, and didn't live here. They've been dead for years. Her father was a gentleman-tailor, worth scores of pounds. And he became a very celebrated bankrupt two or three times."

"Oh, I thought he was quite a common man!" said Joseph.

"Oh, no, no! That man failed for heaps of money; hundreds in gold and silver."

"The daughter was not at all a pretty child," said Henry Fray. "Never should have thought she'd have growed up such a handsome gal as she is."

"'Tis to be hoped her temper is as good as her face."

"Well, yes. But the bailiff will have most to do with the business and ourselves."

While the drinkers were passing the cup, the end of Gabriel Oak's flute became visible sticking out of his pocket, and Henry Fray exclaimed, "Surely, shepherd, I seed you blowing into a great flute at Casterbridge?"

"You did," said Gabriel, blushing faintly. "I've been in great trouble and was driven to it. I used not to be so poor as I be now."

"Never mind!" said Mark Clark. "You should take it careless-like, shepherd, and your time will come. But we could thank ye for a tune, if ye bain't too tired?"

Oak then struck up "Jockey to the Fair," and played that sparkling melody three times through, accenting the notes in the third round in a most artistic and lively manner by bending his body in small jerks and tapping with his foot to beat time.

"He can play the flute very well," said a young married man, who having no individuality worth mentioning, was known as "Susan Tall's husband."

Eventually the men began to file out of the malthouse. Gabriel arose and went off with Jan Coggan, who had offered him a lodging. A few minutes later, when the remaining ones were about to depart, Henry Fray came back again all excited.

"What's the matter, what's the matter, Henry?" said Joseph, starting back.

"What's a-brewing, Henry?" asked Jacob and Mark Clark.

"Bailiff Pennyways—Baily Pennyways—I said so; yes, I said so!"

"What, found out stealing anything?"

"Stealing it is. The news is, that after Miss Everdene got home she went out again to see all was safe, as she usually do, and coming in found Baily Pennyways creeping down the granary steps with half a bushel of barley. She pursued him like a cat. And, to cut a long story short, he owned to having carried off five sacks altogether, upon her promising not to persecute him. Well, she fired him on the spot, and my question is, who's going to be baliff now?"

The question was such a profound one that Henry was obliged to drink there and then from the large cup till the bottom was distinctly visible inside. Before he had replaced it on the table, in came Susan Tall's husband, in a still greater hurry.

"Have ye heard the news that's all over parish?"

"About Baily Pennyways?"

"But besides that?"

"No—not a morsel of it!" they replied.

"Fanny Robin—Miss Everdene's youngest servant—can't be found. They wouldn't be so concerned if she hadn't been noticed in such low spirits these last few days. Well, Miss Everdene wants to speak to one or two of us before we go to bed. What with this trouble about the baliff, and now about the girl, mis'ess is almost wild."

They all hastened up the lane to the farmhouse. From the bedroom window above their heads Bathsheba's head and shoulders, robed in mystic white, were dimly seen.

"Are any of my men among you?" she said anxiously.

"Yes, Ma'am, several," said Susan Tall's husband.

"Tomorrow morning I wish two or three of you to make inquiries in the villages if they have seen such a person as Fanny Robin. Do it quietly; there is no reason for alarm as yet. She must have left while we were all at the fire."

"I beg yer pardon, but had she any young man courting her in the parish, Ma'am?" asked Jacob Smallbury.

"I don't know," said Bathsheba. "What truly worries me is that she was seen to go out of the house by Maryann with only her indoor working gown on—not even a bonnet."

"She had, I think, a bundle, though I couldn't see very well," said a female voice from another window, which seemed that of Maryann. "But she had no young man about here. Hers lives in Casterbridge, and I believe he's a soldier."

"Do you know his name?" Bathsheba said.

"No, mistress. She wouldn't tell anyone who he was."

"Perhaps I might be able to find out if I went to Casterbridge barracks," said William Smallbury.

"Very well. If she doesn't return tomorrow, go there and try to discover which man it is, and see him," Bathsheba said, closing the window.

"Ay, ay, mistress; we will," they replied, and moved away.

That night at Coggan's, Gabriel Oak, beneath the screen of closed eyelids, was busy with fancies, and full of movement, like a river flowing rapidly under its ice. Night had always been the time at which he saw Bathsheba most vividly, and that is how he tenderly regarded her image now. The delight of seeing her in his mind's eye erased, for the time being, his perception of the great difference between seeing and possessing.

CHAPTER 9

The next morning, Bathsheba and her servant-companion, Liddy Smallbury, were sitting upon the floor. There, they were sorting through a collection of papers, books, bottles, and rubbish spread out —remnants from the household stores of the late occupier. Liddy, the maltster's great-granddaughter, was about Bathsheba's equal in age, though not in daring. Both women were in their early twenties.

Through a partly-opened door, the noise of a scrubbing-brush revealed the housekeeper, Maryann Money. "Stop your scrubbing a moment," said Bathsheba through the door to her. "I hear something."

Maryann suspended the brush.

The tramp of a horse was apparent, approaching the front of the building. The door was tapped with the end of a crop or stick.

Mrs. Coggan, the cook, went to the door.

The door opened, and a deep voice said, "Is Miss Everdene at home?"

"I'll see, sir," said Mrs. Coggan, who tramped up the stairs and announced, "Here's Mr. Boldwood wanting to see you, Miss Everdene."

Bathsheba considered her dust-covered face and disorderly clothes. She was hardly prepared to greet a gentleman. "Say I can't see him," she declared.

Mrs. Coggan went downstairs and conveyed this message to the caller.

"Oh, very well," said the deep voice indifferently. "All I wanted to ask was, if anything had been heard of Fanny Robin?"

"Nothing, sir, but we may know tonight. William Smallbury is gone to Casterbridge, where we think her admirer lives, and the other men be inquiring about everywhere."

The horse's tramp then recommenced and retreated, and the door closed.

"Who is Mr. Boldwood?" said Bathsheba.

"A gentleman-farmer at Little Weatherbury."

"Married?"

"No, Miss."

"How old is he?"

"Forty, I should say—very handsome—rather stern-looking—and rich."

"What a bother this dusting is! I am always in some unfortunate situation," Bathsheba complained. "Why should he inquire about Fanny?"

"Oh, because, as she had no supporters in her childhood, he paid for her schooling. Then he got her a job here, working as a servant for your uncle. He's a very kind man. But, oh!"

"What?"

"No woman has ever been able to hold his interest. He's been courted by all the girls around. He cost Farmer Ives's daughter nights of tears and twenty pounds' worth of new clothes. But Lord—

the money might as well have been thrown out of the window."

"What a bother everything is in!" said Bathsheba, discontentedly. "Get away, Maryann, or go on with your scrubbing, or do something! You ought to be married by this time, and not here troubling me!"

"Did anybody ever want to marry you, Miss?" Liddy ventured to ask Bathsheba when they were again alone. "Lots of 'em, I daresay?"

"A man wanted to once," she said, and the image of Gabriel Oak, as the farmer, rose before her.

"How nice it must seem!" said Liddy. "And you wouldn't have him?"

"He wasn't quite good enough for me."

"And did you love him, Miss?"

"Oh, no. But I rather liked him."

"Do you now?"

"Of course not—what footsteps are those I hear?"

Liddy looked from a back window into the courtyard behind, which was now in the shadow of early evening. A crooked file of men was approaching the back door. Two or three women brought up the rear.

"Maryann, go down and keep them in the kitchen till I am dressed properly, and then show them in to me in the hall."

CHAPTER 10

Half an hour later, Bathsheba, followed by Liddy, entered the upper end of the old hall to find that her workers were waiting for her. She sat down at a table and opened the time-book, pen in her hand, with a canvas moneybag beside her.

"Now before I begin, men," said Bathsheba, "I have two matters to speak of. The first is that the bailiff is dismissed for stealing. I have decided to have no bailiff at all, but to manage everything with my own head and hands."

The men breathed an audible breath of amazement.

"The next matter is, have you heard anything of Fanny?"

"Nothing, Ma'am."

"Have you done anything?"

"I met Farmer Boldwood," said Jacob Smallbury, "and I went with him and two of his men, and dragged Newmill Pond, but we found nothing."

"And the new shepherd has been to Buck's Head, by Yalbury, thinking she had gone there, but nobody had seen her," said Laban Tall.

"Hasn't William Smallbury been to Casterbridge?"

"Yes, Ma'am, but he's not yet come home. He promised to be back by six."

"It's a quarter to six at present," said Bathsheba, looking at her watch. "I daresay he'll be in directly. Well, now then"—she looked into the book—"Joseph Poorgrass, are you there?"

"Yes, sir—Ma'am I mean," said the person addressed.

"And what do you do on the farm?"

"I help move things about all the year, and in planting time I shoot the birds that want to eat the seeds. And I help at pig-killing, sir."

"How much money is owed to you?"

"Please, nine and ninepence, sir—Ma'am, I mean."

"Quite correct. Now here are ten shillings in addition as a small present, as I am a newcomer."

In like manner Bathsheba learned the skills of the other workers and paid them their wages.

Closing the book and shaking back a stray curl of hair, Bathsheba inquired, "Has William Smallbury returned?"

"No, Ma'am."

"The new shepherd will want a man under him," suggested Henry Fray.

"Oh—he will. Who can he have?"

"Young Cain Ball is a very good lad," Henry said. "Does Shepherd Oak mind his youth?" he added, turning to the shepherd, who had just appeared on the scene.

"No, I don't mind that," said Gabriel.

"Very well then, Cainey Ball to be under-

shepherd. And you quite understand your duties?—
you, I mean, Gabriel Oak?"

"Quite well, I thank you, Miss Everdene," said
Shepherd Oak. Gabriel was rather staggered by the
remarkable coolness of her manner. Was this the
woman to whom he had once declared his love?
Certainly nobody in the room would have guessed
that Oak and the handsome woman before whom
he stood had ever been other than strangers. But
perhaps her manner was the inevitable result of the
social rise which had advanced her from a cottage to
a large house and fields.

Footsteps were heard in the passage. "Here's
Billy Smallbury come from Casterbridge," several
workers remarked.

"And what's the news?" asked Bathsheba.

"Well, Ma'am, she's run away with the soldiers,"
said William.

"No. Not a steady girl like Fanny!"

"I'll tell ye all particulars. When I got to
Casterbridge Barracks, they said, 'The Eleventh
Dragoon-Guards be gone away, and new troops
have come.' Fanny's young man was one of the
regiment, and she's gone after him. There, Ma'am,
that's it in black and white."

"Did you find out his name?"

"No. Nobody knew it. I believe he was higher
in rank than a private."

Gabriel remained musing and said nothing, for
he was in doubt.

"Well, we are not likely to know more tonight,
at any rate," said Bathsheba. "But one of you had

better run across to Farmer Boldwood's and tell him that much."

She then rose. Before retiring, Bathsheba addressed a few words to the assembled workers. She spoke with a pretty dignity, to which her mourning dress added a seriousness beyond the words themselves.

"Now mind, you have a mistress instead of a master. I don't yet know my powers or my talents in farming. But, I shall do my best. If you serve me well, so shall I serve you. And so goodnight."

"Goodnight, Ma'am," the workers replied.

And so she left.

CHAPTER 11

Our attention shifts to a town and military outpost many miles north of Weatherbury. The night was cold, and a light snow was falling. Beneath the wall of the military outpost, a small shape was moving with difficulty. The bundled mass spoke aloud between labored breaths.

"One. Two. Three. Four. Five."

After each word, the little shape advanced about half a dozen yards. It was evident now that the windows high in the wall were being counted. The word "Five" represented the fifth window from the end of the wall.

Here the figure stooped, gathered some snow together, and flung it toward the fifth window. It smacked against the wall at a point several yards from its mark. Another attempt, and several others, until the wall was pimpled with the adhering lumps of snow. At last one fragment struck the fifth window.

Nothing was heard in reply to the signal. The window was struck again in the same manner.

Then a noise was heard, apparently produced by the opening of the window. This was followed by a masculine voice from the same quarter.

"Who's there?"

"Is it Sergeant Troy?" the girl inquired with much anxiety.

"Yes," came the suspicious reply. "What girl are you?"

"Oh, Frank—don't you know me?" said the figure. "It's your wife, Fanny Robin."

"Fanny!" said the voice, in utter astonishment.

"Yes," said the girl, with a half-suppressed gasp of emotion.

There was something in the woman's tone which was not that of a wife, and there was a manner in the man which is rarely a husband's.

"I did not expect you tonight. Indeed, I did not think you would come at all. It was a wonder you found me here."

"You said I was to come."

"Well—I said that you might."

"Yes, I mean that I might. You are glad to see me, Frank?"

"Oh yes—of course."

"Can you—come to me?"

"My dear Fan, no! The bugle has sounded, the barrack gates are closed, and I cannot leave until morning."

"Then I shan't see you till then!" The words were in a faltering tone of disappointment. "And Frank, when will it be?"

"What?"

"What you promised."

"I don't quite remember."

"Oh, you do! Don't speak like that. It greatly saddens me. It makes me say what ought to be said first by you."

"Never mind—say it."

"Oh, must I?—It is—when shall we be married, Frank? You said lots of times you would marry me, and—and—I—I—I—"

"Don't cry, now! It is foolish. If I said so, of course I will."

"You have the permission of the officers?"

"No, not yet."

"Oh—how is it? You said you almost had before you left Casterbridge."

"The fact is, I forgot to ask. Your coming like this is so sudden and unexpected."

"Yes—yes—it is. It was wrong of me to worry you. I'll go away now. Will you come and see me tomorrow, at Mrs. Twills's, in North Street? I don't like to come to the barracks. There are bad women about, and they think me one."

"Quite, so. I'll come to you, my dear. Goodnight."

"Goodnight, Frank—goodnight!"

The window closed, and the shivering girl moved off into the night. When she passed the corner, a subdued exclamation was heard inside the building.

"Ho—ho—Sergeant—ho—ho!" A reply followed, but it was indistinct; and it became lost amid a low peal of laughter.

CHAPTER 12

The first evidence of Bathsheba's decision to take personal control of the farm was her appearance the following market-day in the corn market at Casterbridge.

At regular intervals, farmers from the surrounding area brought seeds, pigs, cows, sheep and other items to Casterbridge to sell to other farmers who wished to buy. The buying and selling was conducted in a low long hall, known as the Corn Exchange. The building was thronged with men who talked among each other in twos and threes.

Among these earnest traders, a feminine figure glided. She was the only woman present at what was traditionally an all-male gathering. She was prettily and even daintily dressed. At her entry the men ceased talking. Nearly every face was turned toward her.

But Bathsheba had not traveled there to impress men. She had a very practical purpose in mind—to launch her career as a businesswoman. Like the other farmers, she too had her sample-bags. She quickly learned to pour the grains into her hand for inspection by prospective buyers. In arguing over prices, she held to her own firmly, as was natural in a dealer.

Those farmers with whom she had no dealings were continually asking each other, "Who is she?"

The reply would be, "Farmer Everdene's niece; took on Weatherbury Upper Farm; turned away the baily, and swears she'll do everything herself."

The questioner would then shake his head.

"Yes, 'tis a pity she's so headstrong," the first would say. "But we ought to be proud of her here—she lightens up the old place."

Bathsheba was well aware of her power to attract masculine attention. Only one individual among the farmers seemed to pay her no regard whatever. He had a gentlemanly bearing and carried himself with dignity. His face suggested that he was between thirty-five and fifty years of age.

When the buying and selling were finished, Bathsheba rushed off to Liddy, who was waiting for her beside the yellow gig in which they had driven to town. The horse was harnessed to the wagon, and they trotted toward home.

"I've been through it, Liddy, and it is over. I shan't mind it again, for they will all have grown accustomed to seeing me there. This morning it was as bad as being married—eyes everywhere!" But there was one man who didn't notice me at all. A very good-looking man," she continued, "upright; about forty, I should think. Do you know at all who he could be?"

Liddy proclaimed, "I haven't a notion. Besides, what difference does it make, since he paid you no attention."

They bowled along in silence. A low carriage, traveling still more rapidly, overtook and passed them.

"Why, there he is!" Bathsheba said.

Liddy looked. "Him! That's Farmer Boldwood, the man you couldn't see the other day when he called."

"Oh, Farmer Boldwood," murmured Bathsheba, and looked at him as he raced past them. The farmer never turned his head, but kept his eyes fixed on the road ahead, as if Bathsheba and her charms were thin air.

"He's an interesting man—don't you think so?" she remarked.

"Oh yes, very. Everybody says so," replied Liddy.

"I wonder why he is so wrapped up in himself. He seems far away from all he sees around him."

"It is said—but not known for certain—that he met with some bitter disappointment when he was a young man. A woman jilted him, they say."

"People always say that—and we know very well women scarcely ever jilt men; 'tis the men who jilt us. I expect it is simply his nature to be so reserved."

"Simply his nature—I expect so, Miss—nothing else in the world."

"Still, 'tis more romantic to think he has been treated cruelly, poor thing! Perhaps, after all, he has!"

CHAPTER 13

It was Sunday afternoon in the farmhouse, on the thirteenth of February. Lunch being over, Bathsheba asked Liddy to come and sit with her. The moldy house was dreary in wintertime. The atmosphere of the place seemed as old as the walls.

"Did you notice Mr. Boldwood's doings in church this morning, Miss?" Liddy inquired.

"No, indeed," said Bathsheba, with bored indifference.

"His pew is exactly opposite yours, Miss."

"I know it."

"And you did not see his goings-on?"

"Certainly I did not, I tell you. What did he do?"

"Didn't turn his head to look at you once during the entire service."

"Why should he?" demanded her mistress. "I didn't ask him to."

"Oh, no. But everybody else was noticing you, and it was odd he didn't. There, 'tis just like him. Rich and gentlemanly, what does he care?"

"Dear me," Bathsheba blurted out, "I nearly forgot the valentine I bought yesterday."

"Valentine! Who for, Miss?" said Liddy. "Farmer Boldwood?"

"Well, no. It is only for little Teddy Coggan. I have promised him something, and this will be a pretty surprise for him."

Bathsheba took from her desk a gorgeously illuminated card, which she had bought on the previous market-day. In the center was a small oval space. This was left blank, so that the sender might insert a Valentine's Day message.

"What fun it would be to send it to the stupid old Boldwood, and how he would wonder!" said the irrepressible Liddy.

Bathsheba paused to regard the idea at full length. Boldwood's had begun to be a troublesome image—the only man who refused to officially admire her. She was far from being seriously concerned about his nonconformity. Still, it was faintly depressing that the most dignified and valuable man in the parish should withhold his eyes, and that a girl like Liddy should talk about it.

"Really, I don't care particularly to send it to Teddy," remarked her mistress. "He's rather a naughty child sometimes."

"Yes—that he is."

"Let's toss a coin as men do," said Bathsheba, idly. "Now then, head, Boldwood; tail, Teddy. No, we won't toss money on a Sunday. That would be tempting the devil indeed."

"Toss this hymn-book. There can't be no sinfulness in that, Miss."

"Very well. Open, Teddy; shut, Boldwood."

The book went fluttering in the air and came down shut.

Bathsheba took the pen and addressed the card to Boldwood. She left the card unsigned.

"Now, Liddy, we must put a wax seal upon the envelope. Which seal shall we use? Here's one with a motto. I can't read it until I press the seal into the hot wax. We'll use this."

Bathsheba pressed the seal onto the hot wax. She looked closely at the wax to discover the words. "Wonderful!" she exclaimed, throwing down the letter with a hearty giggle.

Liddy looked at the words of the seal, and read— "MARRY ME."

They sent the valentine the same day.

CHAPTER 14

At dusk, on the evening of St. Valentine's Day, Boldwood sat down to supper as usual, by a beaming fire of aged logs. Resting before him was the card Bathsheba had sent. Boldwood, of course, did not know who the sender was. The envelope served as a magnet that attracted the bachelor's gaze wherever his eyes might wander.

"MARRY ME."

When Boldwood went to bed, he placed the valentine in the corner of the large mirror in his room. He was conscious of its presence, even when his back was turned upon it. It was the first time in Boldwood's life that such an event had occurred. Somebody's—some WOMAN'S—hand had traveled softly over the paper bearing his name. He passed a fitful night, wondering who might have sent him the card.

Next morning, Boldwood descended the stairs and went outside. He was listlessly noting how the frost had hardened and glazed the surface of the snow, when he heard the half-muffled noise of the mail-cart approaching. The driver held out a letter. Boldwood seized it and opened it, expecting another anonymous card or letter.

"I don't think it is for you, sir," said the mailman,

surprised by Boldwood's rapid movement. "Though there is no name, I think it is for your shepherd."

Boldwood looked then at the address, which was "To the New Shepherd, Weatherbury Farm, Near Casterbridge."

"Oh, what a mistake!" Boldwood exclaimed. "It is not mine. Nor is it for my shepherd. It is for Miss Everdene's. You had better take it on to him— Gabriel Oak—and say I opened it by mistake."

At this moment, on the ridge, up against the early morning sky, a figure was visible. A small figure on all fours followed behind. The tall form was that of Gabriel Oak; the small one that of his dog, George.

"Wait," said Boldwood. "That's the man on the hill. I'll take the letter to him myself." Boldwood started to make his way through the crunchy snow in the direction of the shepherd.

Oak himself was on the move, marching toward Warren's Malthouse. Boldwood followed at a distance.

CHAPTER 15

The maltster, after having lain down in his clothes for a few hours, was now sitting beside a three-legged table, breakfasting on bread and bacon. Henry Fray, Matthew Moon, Joseph Poorgrass, and other carters and wagoners were present. Great lanterns dangled from their hands, which showed that they had just come from the cart-horse stables, where they had been busily engaged since four o'clock that morning.

"And how is she getting on without a baily?" the maltster inquired. Henry shook his head.

"She'll regret it—surely, surely!" he said. "Benjy Pennyways were not an honest baily—as big a betrayer as Judas Iscariot himself. But to think she can carry on alone!"

"All will be ruined, and ourselves too," said Mark Clark. "A headstrong maid, that's what she is—and won't listen to no advice at all."

A firm loud tread was now heard stamping outside. The door was opened about six inches, and somebody on the other side exclaimed, "Neighbors, have ye got room for a few new-born lambs?"

"Ay, sure, shepherd," said the men inside.

The door was flung back till it smacked the wall and trembled from top to bottom with the blow.

Mr. Oak appeared in the entry with a steaming face. Four lambs hung over his shoulders, and the dog George stalked solemnly behind.

"Well, Shepherd Oak, and how's lambing this year, if I mght ask?" inquired Joseph Poorgrass.

"Terrible trying," said Oak. "I've been soaked through twice-a-day, either in snow or rain, this last fortnight. Cainy and I didn't sleep at all last night."

The maltster broke in. "They've been talking but now of Miss Everdene's strange behavior. No bailiff!"

"What have you been saying about her?" inquired Oak, sharply turning to the rest, and getting very warm.

"They've been a-saying she has too much pride and vanity," said Mark Clark.

Gabriel, though one of the quietest and most gentle men on earth, rose to the occasion. "Look here, neighbors!" he shouted. "That's my fist." Here he placed his fist in the center of the maltster's little table. "Now, the first man that I hear speakin' bad of our mistress, why,"—here the fist was raised and let fall like a mighty hammer—"he'll smell and taste that!" The dog George looked up at the same time after the shepherd's threat. Though he understood English but imperfectly, he began to growl.

"Now, don't ye take on so, shepherd, and sit down!" said Henry, and the conversation resumed its civil tone.

The warmth of the fire now began to stimulate the nearly lifeless newborn lambs to bleat and move their limbs briskly upon the hay, and to recognize for the first time the fact that they were born. Their noise increased to a chorus of 'baas.' This prompted Oak to place a spout of warm milk in each of their mouths. With amazing swiftness, they learned to drink.

At this point, Boldwood entered the malthouse.

"Ah! Oak, I thought you were here," he said. "I met the mail-cart ten minutes ago, and a letter was put into my hand, which I opened without reading the address. I believe it is yours. You must excuse the accident, please."

"Don't think twice about it, Mr. Boldwood—not at all," said Gabriel. He could not imagine who might be writing to him.

Oak stepped aside, and read the following in an unknown hand:

Dear Friend,

I do not know your name, and I hope these few lines will reach you. I write to thank you for your kindness to me the night I left Weatherbury in a reckless way. I also return the money I owe you, which you will excuse my not keeping as a gift. All has ended well. I am happy to say I am going to be married to the young man who has courted me for some time—Sergeant Troy, of the 11th Dragoon Guards, now quartered in this town. He is a man of great respectability and high honor—indeed, a nobleman by blood.

I should be much obliged to you if you would keep the contents of this letter a secret for the present, dear friend. We mean to surprise Weatherbury by coming there soon as husband and wife. Thanking you again for your kindness,

I am your sincere well-wisher,
Fanny Robin

"Have you read it, Mr. Boldwood?" said Gabriel. "If not, you had better do so. I know you are interested in Fanny Robin."

Boldwood read the letter and looked troubled. "Fanny—poor Fanny! The end she is so confident of has not yet come, and may never come. I see she gives no address."

"What sort of a man is this Sergeant Troy?" said Gabriel.

"H'm—I'm afraid not one to build much hope upon," the farmer murmured, "though he's a clever fellow. His mother was a French governess, and it seems that a secret attachment existed between her and the late Lord Severn. She married a poor medical man, and soon after, an infant was born. While money was plentiful, all went well. Unfortunately for her boy, the money ran out. So he took a position as second clerk at a lawyer's in Casterbridge. He stayed there for some time, and showed promise of advancing in the firm. However, he then astonished everyone by enlisting in the cavalry. I have much doubt if ever little Fanny will surprise us in the way she mentions—very much doubt."

The door burst open again, and in ran Cainy Ball, out of breath.

"What have you come for, Cainy?" inquired Oak.

"I've run to tell ye," said the junior shepherd, "that you must come directly. Two more ewes have given birth to twins—that's what's the matter, Shepherd Oak."

"Oh, that's it," said Oak, jumping up, and dismissing for the present his thoughts on poor Fanny. Oak and Cainy hurried in the direction of the lambing field.

Boldwood followed them and caught up with Oak. He drew out the unsigned card and showed the envelope to the shepherd.

"I was going to ask you, Oak," he said, with pretended carelessness, "if you know whose writing this is?"

Oak glanced at the envelope and replied instantly, with a flushed face, "Miss Everdene's."

Soon parting from Gabriel, the lonely and reserved man returned to his house to breakfast. He again placed the letter on the mantelpiece, and sat down to think about these strange circumstances.

Chapter 16

On a weekday morning a small group of worshippers, mainly women and girls, rose from their knees in the moldy nave of a church called All Saints'. The church was located in the town where the 11th Dragoon Guards were quartered. As the service had ended, the worshippers were about to leave. Their progress was halted, however, by the sound of footsteps coming up the central passage. The step echoed with a ring unusual in a church. It was the clink of spurs. Everybody looked. A young cavalry soldier in a red uniform, with the three stripes of a sergeant upon his sleeve, strode up the aisle. He did not pause until he came close to the altar railing. Here for a moment he stood alone.

The officiating curate, who had not removed his religious garb, perceived the newcomer and followed him to the communion-space. He whispered to the soldier, and then beckoned to the clerk. He, in his turn, whispered to an elderly woman, apparently his wife, and they also went up the chancel steps.

"'Tis a wedding!" murmured some of the women, brightening. "Let's wait!"

The majority again sat down.

The soldier and church officials remained together for some time.

"Where's the woman?" whispered some of the spectators.

The young sergeant stood still and remained grimly silent. The minutes went on, and nobody else appeared.

"I wonder where the woman is!" a voice whispered again.

At length the soldier, a cold look upon his face, turned and marched briskly down the aisle and out of the church. Some of the women giggled softly as he passed them.

In front of the church was a paved square, around which several aged wood buildings were situated. The young man on leaving the door went to cross the square. There, in the middle, he met a little woman. Her face reflected intense anxiety. But this expression turned to terror when she beheld the look on the soldier's face.

"Well?" he said, his fury barely contained.

"Oh, Frank—I made a mistake!—I thought that church with the spire was All Saints', and I was at the door at half-past eleven as you said. I waited till a quarter to twelve, and found then that I was in All Souls'. But I wasn't much frightened, for I thought it could be tomorrow as well."

"You fool, for so fooling me! Say no more."

"Shall we get married tomorrow, Frank?" she asked blankly.

"Tomorrow!" he exclaimed with a hoarse laugh. "I won't go through that experience again for some time, I assure you!"

"But consider," she said in a trembling voice, "the mistake was not such a terrible thing! Now, dear Frank, when shall it be?"

"Ah, when? God knows!" he said and, turning from her, walked rapidly away.

CHAPTER 17

On Saturday Boldwood was in Casterbridge market-house as usual, when the disturber of his dreams entered and became visible to him. The farmer took courage, and for the first time really looked at Bathsheba.

To Boldwood, women had been remote beings rather than familiar acquaintances. He had never given thought to whether the orbits of these comets were as regular and unchangeable as his own, or as absolutely erratic as they appeared to be.

Boldwood saw her black hair, her correct facial curves and profile, and the roundness of her chin and throat. He then saw her eyelids, eyes, and lashes, and the shape of her ear. Next he noticed her figure, her skirt, and the very soles of her shoes. He thought her beautiful. It must be remembered that Boldwood, though forty years of age, had never before looked at a woman with such intensity.

Was she really beautiful? He could not assure himself that his opinion was true even now. He quietly said to another farmer, "Is Miss Everdene considered handsome?"

"Oh yes. She was a good deal noticed the first time she came, if you remember. A very handsome girl indeed."

Boldwood was satisfied now.

And this charming woman had in effect said to him, "Marry me." Why should she have done that strange thing? Boldwood had as little idea of the cause of her action as did Bathsheba of what could happen as a result.

Bathsheba was at this moment coolly dealing with a dashing young farmer, adding up the amount he owed her. Boldwood grew hot with jealousy. His first impulse was to go and thrust himself between them. He quickly dismissed this idea as unreasonable.

All this time, Bathsheba was aware that Boldwood's eyes were following her everywhere. This was a triumph for her. Had it come naturally, such a triumph would have been sweet. She genuinely regretted that she had ever played a prank on the unsuspecting gentleman farmer, whom she respected too highly to deliberately tease.

That day, Bathsheba nearly decided to beg Boldwood's pardon at their next meeting, but then had second thoughts. If he thought she was making fun of him, an apology would make the offence worse. However, if he thought she wanted him to woo her, it would read like additional evidence of her forwardness.

CHAPTER 18

Boldwood was the owner of what was called Little Weatherbury Farm. He was the nearest approach to aristocracy that this remote region could boast of.

His house stood back from the road. The stables, which are to a farm what a fireplace is to a room, were behind. Inside the blue door were to be seen at this time the backs and tails of half a dozen warm and contented horses standing in their stalls.

Pacing up and down at the heels of the animals was Farmer Boldwood himself. This place was his refuge. Here, after looking to the feeding of his four-footed dependents, he would walk and meditate in the evening until the moon rose high.

His was not an ordinary nature. If an emotion possessed him at all, it ruled him. A feeling that did not master him was not felt at all. There was nothing light or casual about him. Unmindful of life's occasional follies, he was a serious and earnest man.

Bathsheba had no idea that the recipient of her valentine felt things so intensely. Had she known Boldwood's capacity for deep feelings, she would have been consumed with guilt at what she had done. Indeed, had she known her present power over him, she would have trembled at her responsibility.

Farmer Boldwood came to the stable door and looked across the level fields. Beyond the first enclosure was a hedge, and on the other side of this a meadow belonging to Bathsheba's farm.

It was now early spring—the time of taking the sheep out to munch on the new-sprouted grass. It was that period when the plant world begins to move and swell and the saps to rise. Boldwood, looking into the distant meadows, saw there three figures. They were those of Miss Everdene, Shepherd Oak, and Cainy Ball. When Bathsheba's figure shone upon the farmer's eyes, it lighted him up the way the moon lights up a great tower. At last he decided to go across and speak to her.

He approached the gate of the meadow. Beyond it Bathsheba and Oak were engaged in the operation of making a lamb "take." This occurs whenever an ewe has lost her own offspring. One of the twins of another ewe is given to her as a substitute. Gabriel had skinned the dead lamb, and was tying the skin over the body of the live lamb. Bathsheba was holding open a little pen into which the mother and lamb were driven. Hopefully, the old sheep would develop an affection for the young one.

Bathsheba looked up at the completion of the procedure and saw Farmer Boldwood by the gate. Oak noticed him too. Boldwood felt flustered and decided not to pay Bathsheba a visit after all. Thus, he walked on, hoping that neither would recognize that he had originally intended to enter their field. He passed by without so much as a casual greeting.

As for Bathsheba, she was not deceived into the belief that Farmer Boldwood had walked by on business or in idleness. She concluded that she was herself responsible for Boldwood's appearance there. It troubled her much to see what a great flame a little wildfire was likely to kindle. Bathsheba was no schemer for marriage, nor was she deliberately a trifler with the affections of men. She resolved never again, by look or by sign, to encourage Boldwood in the belief that she cared for him.

CHAPTER 19

It was now the end of May. By this time, Boldwood had grown used to being in love. He had observed Bathsheba from a distance; he had not yet spoken to her. So now he was determined to speak to Bathsheba. On inquiring for her at her house, he was told she was at the sheep-washing, and he went off to seek her there.

The sheep-washing pool was a circular basin of water in the midst of a meadow. Shepherd Oak, Jan Coggan, Moon, Poorgrass, Cain Ball, and several others were assembled here, all dripping wet. Bathsheba was standing by in a new riding-habit—the most elegant she had ever worn. The meek sheep were pushed into the pool by Coggan and Matthew Moon. Then Gabriel pushed them under, with an instrument like a crutch, as they swam along. The sheep were then hauled out of the water, their wool scoured clean of any impurities.

Boldwood came close and wished her good morning, speaking in a very formal manner. Bathsheba immediately started to walk away, but Boldwood was determined to speak to her.

"Miss Everdene!" said the farmer.

She trembled, turned, and said "Good morning."

"I feel—almost too much—to think," he said. "My life is not my own since I first saw you, Miss Everdene. I come to make you an offer of marriage."

Bathsheba tried to remain unmoved by these words.

"I am now forty-one years old," he went on. "All my life I have thought of myself as a confirmed bachelor. But we all change, and I have changed since seeing you. I want you as my wife."

"Oh, Mr. Boldwood. Though I respect you much, I do not feel—what would justify me to—accept your offer," she stammered.

"My life is a burden without you," he exclaimed, in a low voice. "I want you to let me say 'I love you' again and again! I wish I could say courteous flatteries to you," the farmer continued, "but I lack the ability to form such words. I want you for my wife—so wildly that no other feeling can satisfy me. I would never say these things had I not been led to hope."

"The valentine again! Oh that valentine!" she said to herself.

"If you can love me, say so, Miss Everdene. If not—don't say no!"

"Mr. Boldwood, I am afraid I can't marry you, much as I respect you. You are too dignified for me to suit you, sir."

"But, Miss Everdene!"

" I—I didn't—I ought never to have sent you that valentine. Please forgive me. It was a frivolous act that no woman with any self-respect should have done. If you will only pardon my thoughtlessness, I promise never to—"

"No, no, no. Don't say thoughtlessness! Make me think it was the beginning of a feeling that you would love me. You torture me to say it was done in thoughtlessness."

"I have not fallen in love with you, Mr. Boldwood."

"But think. I will take more care of you than would many a man of your own age. I will protect and cherish you with all my strength—I will indeed! You shall have no cares, be worried by no household affairs, and live quite at ease. The dairy superintendence shall be done by a man—I can afford it well—you shall never have so much as to look out of doors at haymaking time, or to think of weather in the harvest. If you like, you shall have a pony-carriage of your own. God only knows how much you are to me!"

Bathsheba's heart swelled with sympathy for the love-stricken man who spoke with so much feeling.

"Don't say any more! Don't! I cannot bear you to feel so much, and me to feel nothing. And I am afraid the men will notice us, Mr. Boldwood. Will you let the matter rest now? I cannot think clearly. I did not know you were going to say this to me. Oh, I am wicked to have made you suffer so!"

"Say then, that you don't absolutely refuse."

"I cannot answer."

"I may speak to you again on the subject?"

"Yes."

"I may think of you?"

"Yes, I suppose you may think of me."

"And hope to obtain you?"

"No—do not hope! I must go."

"I will call upon you again tomorrow."

"No—please not. Give me time."

"Yes—I will give you any time," he said earnestly and gratefully. "I am happier now."

"No—I beg you! Don't be happier if happiness only comes from my agreeing."

"I will wait," he said.

And then she turned and led the horse away. Boldwood dropped his gaze to the ground, and stood there for a long time, like a man who did not know where he was.

CHAPTER 20

"He is so unselfish and kind to offer me all that I can desire," Bathsheba mused.

Yet Farmer Boldwood did not exercise kindness here. The rarest offerings of the purest loves are self-indulgent, and no generosity at all.

Bathsheba, not being the least in love with him, was eventually able to look calmly at his offer. It was one which many women of her own station in the district would have been wild to accept. It made perfect sense that she, a lonely girl, should marry, and marry this earnest, well-to-do, and respected man. He lived close by; his social status was sufficient: his good qualities were beyond question. Also, she had a strong feeling that, having been the one who began the game, she ought in honesty to accept the consequences. Still, her reluctance remained. She esteemed and liked him, yet she did not want him. Besides, Bathsheba's position as absolute mistress of a farm and house was still new to her, and the novelty had not yet begun to wear off.

The next day she found Gabriel Oak at the bottom of her garden, grinding his shears for the sheep-shearing. Cainy Ball turned the handle of Gabriel's grindstone, while Oak held the blades against it.

Bathsheba came up and looked upon them in silence for a minute or two. Then she said, "Cain, go to the lower field and catch the bay mare. I'll turn the winch of the grindstone. I want to speak to you, Gabriel."

Cain departed, and Bathsheba took the handle. Bathsheba turned the winch, and Gabriel applied the shears.

"I wanted to ask you if the men made any observations about my speaking with Mr. Boldwood yesterday?"

"Yes, they did," said Gabriel.

"What did they say?"

"That you and Farmer Boldwood would be married before the end of the year."

"I thought so! There's nothing in it. A more foolish remark was never made, and I want you to contradict it! That's what I came for."

Gabriel looked sad, but relieved.

"They must have heard our conversation," she continued.

"Well, then, Bathsheba!" said Oak, stopping the handle and gazing into her face with astonishment.

"Miss Everdene, you mean," she said, with dignity.

"I mean this, that if Mr. Boldwood really spoke of marriage, I won't lie and say he didn't just to please you. I have already tried to please you too much for my own good!"

Bathsheba looked at Gabriel in confusion. She did not know whether to pity him for his disappointed love of her, or to be angry with him for having gotten over it.

"I said I wanted you just to mention that it was not true I was going to be married to him," she murmured.

"I can say that to them if you wish, Miss Everdene. And I could likewise give an opinion to you on what you have done."

The only opinion on herself and her doings that she valued as sounder than her own was Gabriel Oak's. "Well, what is your opinion of my conduct?" she said, quietly.

"That it is unworthy of any woman of quality."

In an instant Bathsheba's face colored an angry crimson shade.

"I may ask, I suppose, where in particular my unworthiness lies? In my not marrying you, perhaps!"

"Not by any means," said Gabriel quietly. "I have long given up thinking of that matter."

"Or wishing it, I suppose," she said. She secretly expected him to deny this assumption.

Whatever Gabriel felt, he coolly echoed her words, "Or wishing it either." He went on. "My opinion is, since you ask it, that you are greatly to blame for playing pranks upon a man like Mr. Boldwood, merely as a pastime. Leading on a man you don't care for is not a praiseworthy action."

Bathsheba looked up at Gabriel.

"I cannot allow any man to—to criticize my private conduct!" she exclaimed. "Nor will I for a minute. So you'll please leave the farm at the end of the week!"

"Very well, so I will," said Gabriel calmly. He had been held to her by a beautiful thread which it pained him to spoil by breaking, rather than by a chain he could not break. "I should be even better pleased to go at once," he added.

"Go at once then, in Heaven's name!" said she, her eyes flashing at his, though never meeting them. "Don't let me see your face anymore."

"Very well, Miss Everdene—so it shall be."

And he took his shears and went away from her in quiet dignity.

CHAPTER 21

Gabriel Oak had been gone only twenty-four hours when an emergency struck. On Sunday afternoon, Joseph Poorgrass, Matthew Moon, Fray, and half a dozen others came running up to Bathsheba's house.

"Whatever is the matter, men?" she said, meeting them at the door just as she was coming out on her way to church.

"—Sheep have broke fence," said Fray.

"—And got into a field of young clover," said Tall.

"Eating clover kills 'em," said Henry Fray.

"They'll all die if they're not got out and cured!" said Tall.

"That's enough—that's enough!—Oh, you fools!" she cried, throwing her prayer-book into the passage, and running out of doors. "To come to me, and not go and get them out directly! Oh, the idiots!"

Her eyes were at their darkest and brightest now. Since Bathsheba's beauty belonged more to the demonic than to the angelic school, she never looked so well as when she was angry.

All the farm hands ran after her to the clover-field. Most of the afflicted animals were lying down, and could not be stirred. These were bodily lifted out. The others were driven into the adjoining field. Here, after the lapse of a few minutes, several more fell down and lay helpless.

Bathsheba, with a sad, bursting heart, looked at her flock. Many of them foamed at the mouth, their breathing being quick and short. The bellies of all were fearfully swollen.

"Oh, what can I do, what can I do!" said Bathsheba, helplessly.

"There's only one way of saving them," said Tall.

"What way? Tell me quick!"

"They must be pierced in the side with an instrument made for that purpose. 'Tis a hollow pipe, with a sharp pricker inside."

"Can you do it? Can I?"

"No, Ma'am. We can't, nor you neither. It must be done in a particular spot. If ye go to the right or left but an inch, you stab the ewe and kill her. Not even a shepherd can do it, as a rule."

"Then they must die," she said, in a resigned tone.

"Only one man in the neighborhood knows the way," said Joseph, now just come up. "He could cure 'em all if he were here."

"Who is he? Let's get him!"

"Shepherd Oak," said Matthew.

"How dare you name that man in my presence!" she said excitedly. "I told you never to mention him. Never will I send for him—never!"

One of the ewes contracted its muscles horribly, extended itself, and jumped high into the air. The ewe fell heavily, and lay still.

Bathsheba went up to it. The sheep was dead.

"Oh, what shall I do—what shall I do!" she again exclaimed, wringing her hands. "I won't send for him. No, I won't!"

However, the "No, I won't" of Bathsheba meant virtually, "I think I must."

She called out to Laban, "Where is Oak staying?"

"Across the valley at Nest Cottage!"

"Jump on the bay mare, and ride across, and say he must return instantly—that I order him to."

Tall mounted a horse and scrambled off to the cottage. Many minutes passed, and more sheep keeled over. At length, a horse and rider appeared in the distance. As the horse approached, Bathsheba was amazed to see Tall in the saddle.

"Well?" said Bathsheba.

"He says beggars mustn't be choosers," replied Laban.

"What!" said the infuriated Bathsheba.

"He says he shall not come unless you request in a more civil tone, as becomes any woman begging a favor."

"Oh, oh, that's his answer? Who does he think he is? Who am I, then, to be treated like that? Shall I beg to a man who has begged to me?"

Another of the flock sprang into the air, and fell dead. The men looked grave.

Bathsheba burst out crying bitterly. Eventually getting a grip on herself, she instructed Tall to accompany her into the house. Here she sat down and hastily scribbled a polite request for Oak to assist her. At the bottom of the note she wrote, "DO NOT DESERT ME, GABRIEL!"

She gave Tall the note and told him to ride directly to Oak's cottage.

An anxious quarter of an hour passed before the horse's tramp was heard again. Bathsheba was too upset to look up immediately. When she did, she saw Oak atop the mare. Bathsheba looked at him gratefully, and she said, "Oh, Gabriel, how could you serve me so unkindly!"

He muttered a confused reply, and Bathsheba followed him to the field.

Gabriel was already among the rigid, prostrate forms. He had flung off his coat, rolled up his shirtsleeves, and taken from his pocket a small tube with a sharp point. Gabriel began to use it with a dexterity that would have graced a hospital surgeon. Passing his hand over the sheep's left flank, and selecting the proper place, he punctured the skin and outer stomach. Then he suddenly withdrew the point, leaving the tube in its place. A current of air rushed up the tube, and the sheep was saved.

Because he had to hurry, since some of the flock were far gone, Gabriel missed his aim in one case only, striking wide of the mark, and killing the suffering ewe. But of the fifty-seven sheep that had strayed and injured themselves, fifty-two survived;

four had already died, forty-nine operations were successfully performed, and three recovered without an operation.

When Oak had finished his work, Bathsheba came and looked him in the face. "Gabriel, will you stay on with me?" she said, smiling winningly.

"I will," said Gabriel.

And she smiled at him again.

CHAPTER 22

It was the first day of June, and the sheep-shearing season was at its height. On Bathsheba's farm, the shearing was done in the great barn. Overseeing the process was Bathsheba. She carefully watched to see that there was no wounding of the sheep through carelessness, and that the animals were shorn close. Gabriel divided his time between supervising the other shearers and doing the shearing himself.

Bathsheba walked over to where Oak was shearing. He felt more than content in having her watch him, her eyes critically regarding his skillful shears.

"Well done, and done quickly!" said Bathsheba, looking at her watch as the last snip resounded.

"How long, Miss?" said Gabriel, wiping his brow.

"Twenty-three and a half minutes since you took the first lock from its forehead. It is the first time that I have ever seen one done in less than half an hour."

Oak's hope that she was going to stand pleasantly by and time him through another performance was painfully interrupted by Farmer Boldwood's appearance in the barn. He crossed over toward Bathsheba, who turned to greet him. They spoke in low tones. Then Bathsheba left the barn alone, only to reappear in her new green riding-habit. Young Bob Coggan led her mare. Boldwood fetched his own horse from the tree under which it had been tied.

Oak could not ignore them; and in attempting to continue his shearing at the same time that he watched Boldwood's manner, he snipped the sheep in the groin. The animal plunged; Bathsheba instantly gazed towards it, and saw the blood.

"Oh, Gabriel!" she exclaimed, "you who are so strict with the other men—see what you are doing yourself!"

To an outsider, there was not much to complain of in this remark. Oak, however, knew Bathsheba was well aware that she herself was the cause of the poor ewe's wound, because she had wounded the ewe's shearer in a still more vital part. It had a sting which the abiding sense of his inferiority to both herself and Boldwood was not calculated to heal. But he had resolved that he had no longer a lover's interest in her, and so he concealed his feelings.

Boldwood gently helped Bathsheba into the saddle. Before they set off, she called out to Oak.

"I am going now to see Mr. Boldwood's flock of Leicesters. Take my place in the barn, Gabriel, and keep the men carefully to their work."

The horses' heads were turned around, and they trotted away.

"That means a marriage is just around the corner," said Temperance Miller, one of the women who worked on the farm.

"I reckon that's the size o't," said Coggan.

CHAPTER 23

That night, a grand supper was served to all the hands to mark the completion of the shearing for the year. Bathsheba sat at one end of the table. She was unusually excited, her red cheeks and lips glowing. Boldwood was also in attendance. The gentleman-farmer was dressed in cheerful style, in a new coat and white vest. He seemed unusually happy and talkative.

After the extensive meal, several of the workmen sang country songs. Laughter and gaiety flowed around the long table.

Next came the question of the evening. Would Miss Everdene sing to them the song she always sang so charmingly—"The Banks of Allan Water"—before they went home?

After a moment's consideration Bathsheba assented, beckoning to Gabriel.

"Have you brought your flute?" she whispered.

"Yes, Miss."

"Play to my singing, then."

Flanked by Oak and Boldwood, Bathsheba sang in a clear and lovely voice. Subsequent events caused one of the verses to be remembered for many

months, and even years, by more than one of those who were gathered there.

> For his bride a soldier sought her,
> And a winning voice had he.
> On the banks of Allan Water
> None was gay as she!

Bathsheba then wished them goodnight and withdrew. Boldwood joined her in the living room. Oak wandered away under the quiet and scented trees. The shearers rose to leave.

Miss Everdene and Boldwood were alone. Her cheeks had lost a great deal of their healthful fire from the very seriousness of her position. However, her eye was bright with the excitement of a triumph—though it was a triumph which had rather been contemplated than desired.

She was standing behind a low armchair, from which she had just risen. He was kneeling in it—inclining himself over its back toward her, and holding her hand in both his own.

"I will try to love you," she was saying, in a trembling voice quite unlike her usual self-confidence. "And if I can believe that I shall make you a good wife, I shall be willing to marry you. But, Mr. Boldwood, hesitation on so high a matter is honorable in any woman, and I don't want to give a solemn promise tonight. I would rather ask you to wait a few weeks till I can see my situation better."

"But you have every reason to believe that then—"

"I have every reason to hope that at the end of the five or six weeks, I shall be able to promise to be your wife," she said, firmly. "But remember this distinctly. I don't promise yet."

"It is enough. I don't ask more. I can wait on those dear words. And now, Miss Everdene, goodnight!"

"Goodnight," she said, graciously—almost tenderly, and Boldwood withdrew with a serene smile.

Bathsheba knew more of him now; he had entirely bared his heart before her. She was struggling to make amends. To have brought all this about was terrible; but after a while the situation also held a fearful joy.

CHAPTER 24

Among the duties which Bathsheba had voluntarily imposed upon herself, by dispensing with the services of a bailiff, was checking the homestead before going to bed. She did this every evening, to see that all was right and safe for the night. Gabriel usually preceded her in this tour, watching her affairs as carefully as any official bailiff could have done. However, Bathsheba was unaware of his tender devotion.

As watching is best done invisibly, Bathsheba usually carried a dark lantern in her hand. Every now and then she turned on the light to examine nooks and corners. After checking the barn, the stables and other outbuildings, Bathsheba made her way back to the house. The path back to her dwelling passed through a dense grove of fir trees. This was the darkest passage in her walk. On the night of the shearing banquet, Bathsheba made her rounds as usual. As she entered the grove of fir trees, she thought she heard footsteps coming from the other direction.

The noise approached, came close, and a figure was apparently on the point of gliding past her when something tugged at her skirt and pinned it forcibly to the ground. This nearly threw Bathsheba off her balance. In recovering she struck against warm clothes and buttons.

A masculine voice spoke out, "Have I hurt you, mate?"

"No," said Bathsheba, attempting to shrink away.

"We have got hitched together somehow, I think."

"Yes. Are you a woman?"

"Yes."

"A lady, I should have said."

"It doesn't matter."

"I am a man."

"Oh!"

Bathsheba softly tugged again, but could not free her skirt.

"Is that a dark lantern you have? I fancy so," said the man.

"Yes."

"If you'll allow me, I'll open it, and set you free."

A hand seized the lantern, the door was opened, the rays burst out from their prison, and Bathsheba beheld her position with astonishment.

The man to whom she was hooked was brilliant in brass and scarlet. He was a soldier. It was immediately apparent that his spur had become entangled in the hem that decorated the skirt of her dress.

The soldier looked at Bathsheba's face. "I'll unfasten you in one moment, Miss," he said, with newborn gallantry.

"Oh no—I can do it, thank you," she hastily replied, and stooped for the performance.

The unfastening was not such a simple affair. The spur had so wound itself among the edge of her skirt, that separation was likely to be a matter of time.

He too stooped. He looked hard into her eyes when she raised them for a moment. Bathsheba looked down again, for his gaze was too strong to be met point-blank with her own. But Bathsheba noticed that he was young and slim, and that he wore three stripes upon his sleeve.

Bathsheba pulled again, but she could not unfasten her skirt.

"You are a prisoner, Miss; it is no use struggling," said the soldier, jokingly. "I must cut your dress if you are in such a hurry."

"Yes—please do!" she exclaimed, helplessly.

"It wouldn't be necessary if you could wait a moment," he said as he unwound part of the hem from the little wheel on his spur. She withdrew her own hand, but, whether by accident or design, he touched it. Bathsheba was annoyed; she hardly knew why.

His unraveling went on, but it seemed as if it would never end. She looked at him again.

"Thank you for the sight of such a beautiful face!" said the young sergeant.

She colored with embarrassment. "'Twas unwillingly shown," she replied stiffly.

"Do but look. I never saw such a tangle!"

"Oh, 'tis shameful of you. You have been

making it worse on purpose to keep me here—you have! I insist upon undoing it. Now, allow me!"

"Certainly, Miss. I am thankful for beauty, even when 'tis thrown to me like a bone to a dog. These moments will be over too soon!"

Bathsheba was wondering whether she could free herself at the risk of leaving her skirt bodily behind her. The thought was too dreadful. The dress—which she had put on to appear stately at the supper—was the best one of her wardrobe; not another in her stock became her so well. What woman in Bathsheba's position, not naturally timid, and within call of her servants, would have bought escape from a dashing soldier at so dear a price?

"All in good time; it will soon be done, I perceive," said her cool friend.

"This trifling provokes, and—and—"

"Not too cruel!"

"—insults me!"

"It is done in order that I may have the pleasure of apologizing to so charming a woman, which I do most humbly, Madam," he said, bowing low.

Bathsheba really did not know what to say.

"I've seen a good many women in my time," continued the young man in a murmur, "but I've never seen a woman so beautiful as you. Take it or leave it—be offended or like it—I don't care."

"Who are you, then, who can so well afford to ignore my opinion?"

"No stranger. Sergeant Troy. I am staying nearby. There! It is undone at last, you see. Your light fingers were more eager than mine. I wish it had been the knot of knots, which cannot be untied!"

She started up, and so did he. Bathsheba moved away, the lantern in her hand, till she could see the redness of his coat no longer.

"Ah, Beauty; good-bye!" he said.

She made no reply and headed briskly for home.

Liddy had just gone to bed. In ascending to her own chamber, Bathsheba opened the girl's door an inch or two, and, panting, said, "Liddy, is any soldier staying in the village—Sergeant somebody— rather gentlemanly for a sergeant, and good looking—a red coat with blue facings?"

"No, Miss. But really it might be Sergeant Troy home on leave, though I have not seen him."

"Yes. That's the name. Had he a moustache— no whiskers or beard?"

"He had."

"What kind of a person is he?"

"Oh! Miss—I blush to say it—an irresponsible man! But also very quick and smart. Such a clever young dandy he is. He was brought up very well, and sent to Casterbridge Grammar School. Learnt all languages while he was there. However, he wasted his talents and enlisted as a soldier. Even then, he rose to be a sergeant without trying at all. And is he really come home, Miss?"

"I believe so. Goodnight, Liddy."

After all, how could a cheerful woman be permanently offended with the man? There are occasions when girls like Bathsheba will put up with a great deal of unconventional behavior. This occurs when they want to be praised, which is often, or when they want to be mastered, which is sometimes. Just now Bathsheba was experiencing both feelings. Clearly she did not think his bold praise an insult now.

It was a fatal omission of Boldwood's that he had never once told her she was beautiful.

CHAPTER 25

Sergeant Troy was one of those individuals who lived entirely in the present. Reluctant to think about the past, he entertained no regrets. He never worried about the future, so he was free of anxieties.

He was moderately truthful toward men, but to women he lied with regularity. He was a fairly well-educated man for one of middle class—exceptionally well-educated for a common soldier. He could in this way be one thing and seem another: for instance, he could speak of love while thinking of dinner; call on the husband while looking at the wife; be eager to pay while intending to owe.

He had been known to observe casually that in dealing with womankind, the only alternative to flattery was cursing and swearing. There was no third method. "Treat them fairly, and you are a lost man," he would say.

A week or two after the shearing was completed, the farms around Weatherbury were busy with haymaking. Bathsheba approached her hayfields and looked over the hedge toward the haymakers. They were involved in swinging scythes, bundling the cut hay, and tossing it upon the wagon.

From behind the wagon a bright scarlet spot emerged. It was the gallant sergeant, who had come haymaking for pleasure. Nobody could deny that he was doing the mistress of the farm real service by this voluntary contribution of his labor at a busy time.

As soon as she had entered the field, Troy saw her. He stuck his pitchfork into the ground and came forward. Bathsheba blushed with half-angry embarrassment as he came to greet her.

Chapter 26

"Ah, Miss Everdene!" said the sergeant, touching his cap. "Little did I think it was you I was speaking to the other night. And yet, if I had reflected, the 'Queen of the Corn-market,' as I heard you so named in Casterbridge yesterday, could be no other woman. I come now to beg your forgiveness a thousand times for having been led by my feelings to express myself too strongly for a stranger. I am no stranger to this place. I assisted your uncle in these fields countless times when I was a lad. I have been doing the same for you today."

"I suppose I must thank you for that, Sergeant Troy," said the Queen of the Corn-market, in an indifferently grateful tone.

The sergeant looked hurt and sad. "Indeed you need not, Miss Everdene," he said. "Why could you think such a thing necessary?"

"I am glad it is not."

"Why? If I may ask without offence."

"Because I don't much want to thank you for anything."

"Oh these intolerable times—that ill-luck should follow a man for honestly telling a woman she is beautiful! I would rather have curses from you than kisses from any other woman."

Bathsheba was absolutely speechless.

"Well," continued Troy, "I suppose there is a praise which is rudeness, and that may be mine. At the same time, there is a treatment which is injustice, and that may be yours. Because a plain blunt man, who has never been taught concealment, speaks out his mind, he's to be condemned. But, I have the sad satisfaction of knowing that my words, whether pleasing or offensive, are unmistakably true."

Bathsheba moved on to hide the beginning of a smile she could not repress. Troy followed her footsteps.

"But—Miss Everdene—you do forgive me?"

"Hardly."

"Why?"

"You say such bold things."

"I said you were beautiful, and I'll say so still, for you are! The most beautiful ever I saw, or may I fall dead this instant!"

"Don't—don't! I won't listen to you," she said, caught between distress at hearing him and a desire to hear more.

"Ah, well, Miss Everdene, you are—pardon my blunt way—you are rather an injury to our race than otherwise."

"How—indeed?" she said, opening wide her eyes.

"Allow me to explain. Probably one man on average falls in love with each ordinary woman. She can marry him: he is content and leads a useful life. Such women as you a hundred men always desire. You can marry only one of that many. Out of these, twenty will seek to drown the bitterness of unanswered love in drink. Twenty more will waste their lives without a wish or attempt to make a mark in the world. That is because they have no ambition apart from their attachment to you. Twenty more, myself possibly among them, will be always pursuing you, getting where they may just see you. The rest may try to get over their passion with more or less success. But all these men will be saddened. And not only those ninety-nine men, but the ninety-nine women they might have married are saddened with them. That's why I say that a woman so charming as yourself, Miss Everdene, is hardly a blessing to her race."

"Ah!" she replied, "if you could only fight half as winningly as you can talk, you would be able to make a pleasure of a bayonet wound!" And then poor Bathsheba instantly perceived her slip in making this admission. "Don't speak to me again in that way, or in any other, unless I speak to you," she said.

"Oh, Miss Bathsheba! That is too hard!"

"No, it isn't. Why is it?"

"You will never speak to me, for I shall not be here long. I am soon going back again to the miserable monotony of drill. And perhaps our regiment will be ordered out soon."

"When are you going from here?" she asked, with some interest.

"In a month."

"But how can it give you pleasure to speak to me?"

"You may think a man foolish to want a mere word—just a good morning. Perhaps he is—I don't know. But you have never been a man looking upon a woman, and that woman yourself."

"Well."

"Then you know nothing of what such an experience is like."

"Nonsense, flatterer! What is it like? I am interested in knowing."

"Put shortly, it is not being able to think, hear, or look in any direction except one without wretchedness, nor there without torture."

"Ah, Sergeant, it won't do—you are pretending!" she said, shaking her head. "Why, you only saw me the other night!"

"That makes no difference. The lightning works instantaneously. I loved you then, at once—as I do now."

"You cannot and you don't," she said demurely. "There is no such sudden feeling in people. I won't listen to you any longer. I wish I knew what time it is. I am going. I have wasted too much time here already!"

The sergeant looked at his watch and told her the time. "What, haven't you a watch, Miss?" he inquired.

"I have not just at present. I am about to get a new one."

"No. You shall be given one. A gift, Miss Everdene—a gift."

And before she knew what the young man was intending, a heavy gold watch was in her hand.

"It is an unusually good one for a man like me to possess," he quietly said. "That watch has a history. It belonged to the last Earl of Severn. It was given to my father, a medical man, for his use till I came of age, when it was given to me. It was all the fortune that ever I inherited. That watch has regulated imperial interests in its time. Now it is yours."

"But, Sergeant Troy, I cannot take this—I cannot!" Bathsheba exclaimed, with round-eyed wonder. "A gold watch!"

The sergeant retreated to avoid receiving back his gift, which she held out toward him.

"Keep it, Miss Everdene, keep it!" said the impulsive sergeant. "The fact of your possessing it makes it worth ten times as much to me. It is in far worthier hands than ever it has been in before."

"But indeed I can't have it!" she said, in a perfect simmer of distress. "Oh, how can you do such a thing?"

"I loved my father, but I love you more. That's how I can do it," said the sergeant.

Bathsheba was brimming with agitation. She exclaimed, "Oh, how can it be that you care for me, and so suddenly! You have seen so little of me. And my workfolk see me following you about the field, and are wondering. Oh, this is dreadful!" she went on.

"Let it be, then, let it be," he said, receiving back the watch. "I must be leaving you now. And will you speak to me for these few weeks of my stay?"

"Indeed I will. Yet, I don't know if I will! Oh, why did you come and disturb me so!"

"Well, will you let me work in your fields?" he coaxed.

"Yes, I suppose so, if it is any pleasure to you."

"Miss Everdene, I thank you."

"No, no."

"Goodbye!"

The sergeant brought his hand to his cap, saluted, and returned to the distant group of haymakers.

Bathsheba could not face the haymakers now. Her heart beating wildly, she retreated homeward, murmuring, "Oh, what have I done! What does it mean! I wish I knew how much of it was true!"

CHAPTER 27

The day after her conversation with Troy, Bathsheba decided to tend the beehives at the farm. She had dressed the hive with herbs and honey, fetched a ladder, brush, and crook, and put on leather gloves, a straw hat, and a large gauze veil. As she was climbing a ladder to reach the hives, she heard, not ten yards off, a voice that was beginning to cause her agitation.

"Miss Everdene, let me assist you. You should not attempt such a thing alone."

Troy was just opening the garden gate.

Bathsheba flung down the brush, crook, and empty hive, pulled the skirt of her dress tightly round her ankles in a tremendous flurry, and as well as she could slid down the ladder. By the time she reached the bottom, Troy was there also, and he stooped to pick up the hive.

"How fortunate I am to have dropped in at this moment!" exclaimed the sergeant.

She found her voice in a minute. "What! And will you give me a hand?" she asked, in a faltering way.

"Why, of course I will. How stunning you are today!" Troy fetched the largest hive down from a tree. "Upon my life," he said, through the veil he put on, "holding up this hive makes one's arm ache worse than a week of sword-exercise."

"I have never seen that demonstrated."

"Would you like to?" said Troy.

Bathsheba hesitated. She had heard wondrous reports of this strange and glorious performance, the sword-exercise. Men and boys who had peeped through chinks or over walls into the barrack-yard returned with accounts of its being the most flashing affair conceivable. So she said mildly what she felt strongly, "Yes; I should like to see it very much."

"And so you shall; you shall see me go through it."

"No! How?"

"Let me consider."

"Not with a walking-stick—I don't care to see that. It must be a real sword."

"Yes, I know; and I have no sword here; but I think I could get one by the evening. Now, will you do this?" Troy bent over her and murmured some suggestion in a low voice.

"Oh no, indeed!" said Bathsheba, blushing. "Thank you very much, but I couldn't on any account."

"Surely you might? Nobody would know."

She shook her head, but weakly. "If I were to," she said, "I must bring Liddy too. Might I not?"

Troy looked far away. "I don't see why you want to bring her," he said coldly.

Bathsheba's eyes betrayed that she also felt that Liddy would be unwanted in the suggested scene.

"Well, I won't bring Liddy—and I'll come. But only for a very short time," she added.

"It will not take five minutes," said Troy. And they chose a place to meet later.

Chapter 28

The hill opposite Bathsheba's dwelling extended, a mile off, into an uncultivated tract of land. At eight o'clock this midsummer evening, the sun still gilded the ferns that decorated the fields. Bathsheba had started out toward her meeting with Troy, but then reversed direction and headed back toward home. Once more, she changed direction and marched toward the meeting place. As she approached the designated spot, she found herself trembling and panting at her audacity. At length she stood on the rim of a pit in the middle of the field. Troy stood in the bottom, looking up toward her.

"I heard you rustling through the ferns before I saw you," he said, coming up and giving her his hand to help her down the slope.

The shallow pit was saucer-shaped, about thirty feet across. The floor was covered with a thick carpet of moss and grass.

Troy produced the sword, which, as he raised it into the sunlight, gleamed a sort of greeting. "First, we have four right and four left cuts; four right and four left thrusts. Our first cut is as if you were sowing your corn." Troy demonstrated the movement. Bathsheba saw a sort of rainbow, upside

down in the air, and Troy's arm was still again. "Cut two, as if you were hedging—so. Three, as if you were reaping—so. Four, as if you were threshing—in that way. Then the same on the left. The thrusts are these: one, two, three, four, right; one, two, three, four, left." He repeated them.

"Next, cuts, points and guards altogether." Troy duly exhibited them.

"Now I'll make it more interesting. You are my foe, with this difference from real warfare, that I shall miss you every time by one hair's breadth. Mind you don't flinch, whatever you do."

"I'll be sure not to!" she said with resolve.

He pointed to about a yard in front of him.

Bathsheba's adventurous spirit was beginning to really enjoy this novel exhibition. She took up her position as directed, facing Troy.

"Now, just to learn whether you have nerve enough to let me do what I wish, I'll give you a preliminary test."

The next thing of which she was conscious was that the point and blade of the sword were darting with a gleam toward her left side, just above her hip. Then, they reappeared on her right side, as if they had passed through her body. Then she saw the same sword held vertically in Troy's hand. All was as quick as electricity.

"Oh!" she cried out, pressing her hand to her side. "Have you run me through?—No, you have not! Whatever have you done?"

"I have not touched you," said Troy, quietly. "It was mere sleight of hand. The sword passed behind you. Now you are not afraid, are you? Because if you are, I can't perform. I give my word that I will not hurt you."

"I don't think I am afraid. You are quite sure you will not hurt me?"

"Quite sure."

"Is the sword very sharp?"

"Oh no—only stand as still as a statue. Now!"

In an instant the atmosphere was transformed in Bathsheba's eyes. Beams of light reflected from Troy's flashing blade, which seemed everywhere at once. These circling gleams were accompanied by a keen rush that was almost a whistling—also springing from all sides of her at once. In short, she was enclosed in a garment of light, and of sharp hisses, resembling a sky-full of meteors close at hand.

The flashing and hissing of the sword finally ceased.

"Wait," he said, breathing hard. "That outer loose lock of hair wants tidying," he said, before she had moved or spoken. "I'll do it for you."

An arc of silver shone on her right side. The sword descended. The lock dropped to the ground.

"Bravely borne!" said Troy. "You didn't flinch a bit. Wonderful in a woman! I won't touch you at all—not even your hair. I am only going to kill that caterpillar settling on you. Now; be still!"

It appeared that a caterpillar had fallen on her shoulder and was resting there, no doubt also impressed by Troy's swordplay. She saw the point glisten toward her shoulder and seemingly enter it. Bathsheba closed her eyes in the full persuasion that she was killed at last. However, feeling no pain, she opened them again.

"There it is, look," said the sergeant, holding his sword before her eyes.

The caterpillar was spitted upon its point.

"Why, it is magic!" said Bathsheba, amazed.

"Oh, no—skill. I merely 'gave point' to your shoulder where the caterpillar was. And instead of running you through, I stopped a thousandth of an inch short of your surface."

"But how could you chop off a curl of my hair with a sword that has no edge?"

"No edge! This sword will shave like a razor. Look here."

He touched the palm of his hand with the blade, and then, lifting it, showed her a thin shaving of skin dangling therefrom.

"But you said before beginning that it was blunt and couldn't cut me!"

"That was to get you to stand still, and so make sure of your safety. The risk of injuring you through your moving was too great not to force me to tell you a fib to escape it."

She shuddered. "I have been within an inch of my life, and didn't know it!"

"More precisely speaking, you have been within half an inch of being sliced alive two hundred and ninety-five times."

"Cruel, cruel, 'tis of you!"

"You have been perfectly safe, nevertheless. My sword never errs." And Troy returned the weapon to the scabbard.

Bathsheba, overcome by a hundred confused feelings, absentmindedly sat down on a tuft of heather. She felt powerless to withstand or deny him. He was altogether too much for her.

"I must leave you now," said Troy, softly. "And I'll venture to take and keep this in remembrance of you."

She saw him stoop to the grass and pick up the lock of hair that he had cut, twist it round his fingers, unfasten a button in his coat, and carefully put it inside. He drew near and said, "I must be leaving you."

He drew nearer still, bent his mouth down toward hers, and kissed her. A minute later she saw his scarlet form disappear into the woods.

That kiss brought the blood beating into her face and set her heart aflame. She felt like one who had sinned a great sin.

CHAPTER 29

We now see the element of foolishness enter the character of Bathsheba Everdene. Although she had too much wisdom to be entirely governed by her emotions, she also had too much emotion to use her wisdom to the best advantage. Bathsheba loved Troy in the way that only self-reliant women love when they abandon their self-reliance. When a strong woman recklessly throws away her strength, she is worse than a weak woman who has never had any strength to throw away. She has never had practice in making the best of such a condition. Weakness is doubly weak by being new.

In one sense, Bathsheba was a woman of the world. However, her world was very limited. She dwelled in a world of green grass and cattle. It was a world where a quiet family of rabbits lives on the other side of the wall, and where calculation is confined to market-days. Of the social conventions of urban fashionable society she knew but little. Her love was like a child's, and though warm as summer, it was fresh as spring. She was not used to weighing her feelings against the counterweight of their consequences.

Furthermore, Troy's deficiencies lay concealed from a woman's vision. In contrast, his attractive qualities burst upon the very surface. He thus differed from homely Oak. His defects were evident to the blindest, while his virtues were as hidden as ore buried underground.

The difference between love and respect was markedly shown in Bathsheba's conduct. Bathsheba had spoken of her interest in Boldwood with the greatest freedom to Liddy, but she had communed only with her own heart concerning Troy.

Gabriel perceived Bathsheba's love-sickness for Troy. It troubled Oak as he worked the farm by day and into the small hours of many a night. That Bathsheba did not love him was his great sorrow. Now his agony was compounded by observing that Bathsheba was in love with someone else.

There is a noble, though usually unsuccessful, kind of love in which not even the fear of inspiring hatred in the loved one can deter someone from trying to save her from error. Oak determined to speak to Bathsheba. He would base his appeal on what he considered her unfair treatment of Farmer Boldwood, now absent from home.

An opportunity occurred one evening when she went for a short walk through the neighboring wheat fields. It was dusk when Oak took the same path and met her returning.

The wheat was now tall, and the path was narrow. Thus the way was quite a sunken groove between the crop on either side. Two persons could not walk abreast without damaging the crop, and Oak stood aside to let her pass.

"Oh, is it Gabriel?" she said. "You are taking a walk too. Goodnight."

"I thought I would come to meet you, as it is rather late," said Oak, turning and following at her heels when she had brushed somewhat quickly by him.

"Thank you, indeed, but I am not very fearful."

"Oh no; but there are bad characters about."

"I never meet them."

Oak had been going to introduce the gallant sergeant as one of these "bad characters." But raising his name here seemed awkward. Oak tried a different tack.

"As the man who would naturally come to meet you is away from home—I mean Farmer Boldwood—why, thinks I, I'll go," he said.

Bathsheba replied rather tartly, "I don't quite understand what you meant by saying that Mr. Boldwood would naturally come to meet me."

"I meant on account of the wedding which they say is likely to take place between you and him, Miss. Forgive my speaking plainly."

"They say what is not true," she responded quickly. "No marriage is likely to take place between us. Since this subject has been mentioned," she said very emphatically, "I am glad of the opportunity of clearing up a mistake which is very common and very provoking. I didn't definitely promise Mr. Boldwood anything. I have never cared for him. I respect him, and he has urged me to marry him. But I have given him no distinct answer. As soon as he returns, I shall do so. The answer will be that I cannot think of marrying him."

"People are full of mistakes, seemingly."

"They are."

Not quite knowing how to raise the subject appropriately, Oak then exclaimed, "I wish you had never met that young Sergeant Troy, Miss."

Bathsheba stopped in her tracks. "Why?" she asked.

"He is not good enough for 'ee."

"Sergeant Troy is an educated man, and quite worthy of any woman. He is well born."

"His being higher in learning and birth than the ordinary soldier is anything but a proof of his worth. It shows his course to be downward."

"Mr. Troy's course is not by any means downward. And his superiority IS a proof of his worth!"

"I believe him to have no conscience at all. And I cannot help begging you, Miss, to have nothing to do with him. Listen to me this once—only this once! I don't say he's such a bad man as I have fancied—I pray to God he is not. But since we don't exactly know what he is, why not behave as if he MIGHT be bad, simply for your own safety? Don't trust him, mistress. I ask you not to trust him so. When he tries to talk to you again, why not turn away with a short 'Good day.' And when you see him coming one way, turn the other. Don't be unmannerly toward him, but harmless-uncivil, and so get rid of the man."

Bathsheba could hardly contain her agitation.

"I say—I say again—that it doesn't become you to talk about him. Why he should be mentioned puzzles me quite!" she exclaimed desperately. "I know this, th-th-that he is a thoroughly conscientious man—blunt sometimes even to rudeness—but always speaking his mind about you plain to your face!"

"Oh."

"He is as good as anybody in this parish! He is very particular, too, about going to church—yes, he is!"

"I am afraid nobody saw him there. I never did, certainly."

"The reason of that is," she said eagerly, "that he goes in privately by the old tower door, just when the service begins, and sits at the back of the gallery. He told me so."

Oak was grieved to find how entirely she trusted Troy. He brimmed with deep feeling as he replied in a steady voice, "You know, mistress, that I love you, and shall love you always. I have lost in the race for money and good things. But Bathsheba, this I beg you to consider—that, both to keep yourself well honored among the workfolk, and in common generosity to an honorable farmer who loves you as much as I, you should be more discreet in your bearing toward this soldier."

"Don't, don't, don't!" she exclaimed, in a choking voice.

"Are you not more to me than my own affairs, and even life?" he went on. "Come, listen to me! I am six years older than you, and Mr. Boldwood is ten years older than I. Consider—I do beg of you to consider before it is too late—how safe you would be in his hands!"

Oak's allusion to his own love for her lessened, to some extent, her anger at his interference. But she could not really forgive him for letting his wish to marry her be eclipsed by his wish to do her good.

"I wish you to go elsewhere," she commanded. "Do not remain on this farm any longer. I don't want you—I beg you to go!"

"That's nonsense," said Oak, calmly. "This is the second time you have pretended to dismiss me. What's the use o' it?"

"Pretended! You shall go, sir—your lecturing I will not hear! I am mistress here."

"Go, indeed—what folly will you say next? Treating me like Dick, Tom and Harry when you know that a short time ago my position was as good as yours! How would the farm go on with nobody to mind it but a woman?"

Bathsheba murmured something to the effect that he might stay if he wished. Then she said more distinctly, "Will you leave me alone now?"

"Certainly I will, Miss Everdene," said Gabriel, gently. He wondered why her request should have come at that moment, for the argument was now over. He stood still and allowed her to get far ahead of him till he could only see her form against the sky.

Oak now perceived Bathsheba's reason for getting free of him at that point in time. A figure appeared beside her. The shape beyond all doubt was Troy's.

Gabriel went home by way of the churchyard. In passing the tower, he thought of what Bathsheba had said about the sergeant's virtuous habit of entering the church by the little gallery door. He climbed up the steps and examined the door. A foot-long sprig of ivy had grown from the wall across the door, delicately tying the panel to the stone jamb. It was a decisive proof that the door had not been opened since Troy came back to Weatherbury.

CHAPTER 30

Half an hour later Bathsheba entered her own house. Her face was flush with excitement. The farewell words of Troy, who had accompanied her to the very door, still lingered in her ears. He had bidden her good-bye for two days, because, he said, he was visiting some friends at Bath. He had also kissed her a second time.

She sank down into a chair, fevered by the evening's events. Then she jumped up with an air of decision and wrote a letter to Boldwood. She wrote that she had well considered his proposal of marriage, and that her final decision was that she could not marry him.

It was impossible to send this letter till the next day. To make sure she would not change her mind, she arose to take the letter to any one of the women who might be in the kitchen. In the passageway, she paused. A dialogue was going on in the kitchen, and Bathsheba and Troy were its topic.

"If he marry her, she'll give up farming."

"'Twill be a gallant life, but may bring some trouble—so say I."

"Well, I wish I had half such a husband."

She burst in upon the women. "Who are you speaking of?" she asked.

There was a pause before anybody replied. At last Liddy said frankly, "What was passing was a bit of a word about yourself, Miss."

"I thought so! Maryann and Liddy and Temperance—I forbid you to suppose such things. You know I don't care the least for Mr. Troy—not I. Everybody knows how much I hate him.—Yes," she repeated, "HATE him!"

"We know you do, Miss," said Liddy; "and so do we all."

"I hate him too," said Maryann.

"Maryann—Oh you lying woman! How can you say such a thing!" said Bathsheba, excitedly. "You admire him greatly, you know it!"

"Yes, Miss, but so did you. He is a wild scamp now, and you are right to hate him."

"He's NOT a wild scamp! How dare you say that to my face! I have no right to hate him, nor you, nor anybody. But who cares! What is it to me what he is? You know it is nothing. I don't care for him. I won't defend his good name, not I. Mind this, if any of you say a word against him, you'll be dismissed instantly!"

She flung down the letter and surged back into the parlor, with a big heart and tearful eyes, Liddy following her.

"Oh, Miss!" said mild Liddy, looking pitifully into Bathsheba's face. "I am sorry we mistook you so! I did think you cared for him. But I see you don't now."

"Shut the door, Liddy."

Liddy closed the door.

Bathsheba burst out: "Oh Liddy, are you such a simpleton? Can't you see? I do love him to distraction and misery and agony! Come closer—closer." She put her arms round Liddy's neck. "I must let it out to somebody. Don't you yet know enough of me to see through that miserable denial of mine? Oh God, what a lie it was! Heaven and my Love forgive me. And don't you know that a woman who loves at all thinks nothing of fibbing when it is balanced against her love? There, go out of the room. I want to be quite alone."

Liddy went toward the door.

"Liddy, come here. Solemnly swear to me that he's not a scoundrel, that it is all lies they say about him!"

"But, Miss, how can I say he is not if—"

"You graceless girl! How can you have the cruel heart to repeat what they say? Unfeeling thing that you are. . . . But I'LL see if you or anybody else in the village, or town either, dare do such a thing!" She started off, pacing from fireplace to door, and back again.

"No, Miss. I don't—I know it is not true!" said Liddy, frightened at Bathsheba's intensity.

"I suppose you only agree with me to please me. But, Liddy, he CANNOT BE bad, as is said. Do you hear?"

"Yes, Miss, yes."

"And you don't believe he is?"

"I don't know what to say, Miss," said Liddy, beginning to cry. "If I say No, you don't believe me. If I say Yes, you rage at me!"

"Say you don't believe it—say you don't!"

"I don't believe him to be so bad as they make out."

"He is not bad at all. . . . My poor life and heart, how weak I am!" Bathsheba moaned. "Oh, how I wish I had never seen him! Loving is misery for women always. I shall never forgive God for making me a woman, and dearly am I beginning to pay for the honor of owning a pretty face." She turned to Liddy suddenly. "Mind this, Lydia Smallbury, if you repeat anywhere a single word of what I have said to you inside this closed door, I'll never trust you, or love you, or have you with me a moment longer—not a moment!"

"I won't repeat anything," sobbed Liddy, "nor will I leave you!"

"I don't often cry, do I, Liddy? But you have made tears come into my eyes," Bathsheba said, a smile shining through the moisture. "Try to think him a good man, won't you, dear Liddy?"

"I will, Miss, indeed."

"He is a steady man in a wild way, you know. That's better than to be as some are, wild in a steady way. I am afraid that's how I am. And promise me to keep my secret—do, Liddy! And do not let them know that I have been crying about him, because it will be dreadful for me, and no good to him, poor thing!"

"I shall never tell a soul, and I'll always be your friend," replied Liddy. "I think God likes us to be good friends, don't you?"

"Indeed I do."

CHAPTER 31

Bathsheba awakened the next morning nervous that Boldwood would return in person to answer her note. Therefore, she set out that afternoon to fulfill an engagement made with Liddy some few hours earlier. Bathsheba's companion, as a token of their friendship, had been granted a week's holiday to visit her sister. The arrangement was that Miss Everdene should journey there for a day or two to inspect some agricultural inventions that Liddy's brother-in-law had fashioned.

Bathsheba went out of the house just at the close of a thundershower, which had bathed the air and freshened the land. Even the birds were singing their approval of the recent scouring.

She had walked nearly two miles when she beheld, advancing over Yalbury hill, the very man she sought so anxiously to avoid. Boldwood was stepping on, but not with that quiet tread of reserved strength which was his customary gait. Instead, his manner was stunned and sluggish now. He looked up at the sound of her footsteps. His changed appearance signaled the effects brought about by her letter.

"Oh, is it you, Mr. Boldwood?" she uttered, a touch of guilt shading her voice.

Those who have the power of communicating in silence sometimes find it a means more effective than words. There are accents in the eye which are not on the tongue. Boldwood's silent look conveyed his thoughts. At length he spoke.

"You know how I feel about you," he said. "No dismissal by a hasty letter affects that."

"I wish you did not feel so strongly about me," she murmured. "It is generous of you, and more than I deserve, but I must not hear it now."

"Hear it? I am not to marry you. Your letter was plain enough."

Bathsheba was anxious to free herself from this fearfully awkward encounter. She confusedly said, "Good evening," and started to move on. Boldwood caught up to her and asked, "Bathsheba—darling—is it final indeed?"

"Indeed it is."

"Oh, Bathsheba—have pity upon me!" Boldwood burst out. "God's sake, yes—I am come to that low, lowest stage—to ask a woman for pity! Still, she is you—she is you. In human mercy to a lonely man, don't throw me off now!"

"I don't throw you off—indeed, how can I? I never loved you." How easily she forgot the valentine she had sent him.

"Bathsheba, if you say you gave me no encouragement, I cannot but contradict you."

"What you call encouragement was the childish game of an idle minute. I have bitterly repented of it—ay, bitterly, and in tears. Must you still go on reminding me?"

"But I took for earnest what you insist was jest. Oh, could I but have foreseen the torture that trifling trick was going to lead me into, how I should have cursed you. But I cannot do that, for I love you too well! Bathsheba, you are the first woman I have ever loved. It is the having been so near claiming you for my own that makes this denial so hard to bear. How nearly you promised me! How dearly you spoke to me behind the spear-bed at the washing-pool, and in the barn at the shearing, and that dearest last time in the evening at your home! Are your pleasant words all gone?"

Bathsheba looked him quietly and clearly in the face, and said in her low, firm voice, "Mr. Boldwood, I promised you nothing. Only a woman of stone would show no tenderness, when a man says he loves her. Please be reasonable, and think more kindly of me!"

"Well, never mind arguing—never mind. One thing is sure: you were all but mine, and now you are not mine. Everything is changed, and that by you alone, remember. You were nothing to me once, and I was contented; you are now nothing to me again, and how different the second nothing is from the first! Would to God you had never taken me up, since it was only to throw me down!"

"I did not take you up—surely I did not!" she answered. "But don't be in this mood with me. I can endure being told I am in the wrong, if you will only tell it to me gently! Oh sir, will you not kindly forgive me, and look at it cheerfully?"

"Cheerfully! Can a man fooled to utter misery

find a reason for being merry? Heavens, you must be heartless. Had I known what was to be, how I would have avoided you! I tell you all this, but what do you care! You don't care."

Bathsheba returned silent and weak denials to his charges, and swayed her head desperately, as if to thrust away the words.

"Dearest, dearest, I am wavering even now between the two opposites of recklessly renouncing you, and laboring humbly for you again. Forget that you have said No, and let it be as it was! Say, Bathsheba, that you only wrote that refusal to me in fun—come, say it to me!"

"It would be untrue, and painful to both of us." She continued, "Good sir, you overrate my capacity for love. I don't possess half the warmth of nature you believe me to have. An unprotected childhood in a cold world has beaten gentleness out of me."

He immediately said, with more resentment, "That will not do. You are not the cold woman you would have me believe. No, no! It isn't because you have no feeling in you that you don't love me. You naturally would have me think so—you would hide from me that you have a burning heart like mine. You have love enough, but it is directed toward someone else. I know who. Why did Troy not leave my treasure alone?" he asked, fiercely. "Before he captured you, your inclination was to have me. Your answer would have been Yes. Can you deny it—I ask, can you deny it?"

"I cannot," she whispered.

"I know you cannot. But he stole in, in my

absence, and robbed me. Now the people sneer at me—the very hills and sky seem to laugh at me. I have lost my respect, my good name, my standing— lost it, never to get it again. Go and marry your man—go on! Dazzled by brass and scarlet—Oh, Bathsheba—this is woman's folly indeed!"

"Oh sir—Mr. Boldwood! It is unmanly to attack a woman so! I have nobody in the world to fight my battles for me. Yet if a thousand of you sneer and say things against me, I WILL NOT be put down!"

"You'll chatter with him doubtless about me. Say to him, 'Boldwood would have died for me.' Yes, and you have given way to him, knowing him to be not the man for you. He has kissed you—claimed you as his. He has kissed you. Deny it!"

"He has," she said, slowly, and, in spite of her fear, defiantly. "I am not ashamed to speak the truth."

"Then curse him, curse him!" said Boldwood, breaking into a whispered fury. "While I would have given worlds to touch your hand, you have let a villain kiss you! Heaven's mercy—kiss you!"

"Don't, don't, oh, don't pray down evil upon him!" she implored in a miserable cry. "Anything but that—anything. Oh, be kind to him, sir, for I love him true!"

The gathering night concentrated itself in Boldwood's eye. "I'll punish him—by my soul, that will I! I'll meet him, soldier or no, and I'll horsewhip the scoundrel for this reckless theft of my one delight. If he were a hundred men, I'd horsewhip him—" He dropped his voice suddenly and unnaturally.

"Bathsheba, sweet, pardon me! I've been blaming you, when he's the greatest sinner. He stole your dear heart away with his unfathomable lies! . . . It is a fortunate thing for him that he's gone back to his regiment—that he's away up the country, and not here! I pray God he may not come into my sight, for I may be tempted beyond myself. Oh, Bathsheba, keep him away—yes, keep him away from me!"

With those words, Boldwood turned his face away and withdrew. His form was soon covered over by the twilight as his footsteps mixed in with the low hiss of the leafy trees.

Bathsheba, who had been standing motionless all this time, flung her hands to her face. In vain, she tried to make sense out of what had just transpired.

The farmer's threats held a special menace for her. Unknown to anyone else, Troy had not returned to his distant barracks as Boldwood and others had supposed. He had merely gone to visit some acquaintance in Bath. He was, in fact, coming back to Weatherbury in the course of the very next day or two. She felt wretchedly certain that if he revisited her now, and came into contact with Boldwood, a fatal quarrel would result.

In her distraction, instead of advancing further, she walked up and down, beating the air with her fingers, pressing on her brow, and sobbing brokenly to herself. Then she sat down on a heap of stones by the wayside to think. There she remained until night fell, but her troubled spirit was far away with Troy.

CHAPTER 32

The village of Weatherbury was quiet as the graveyard in its midst, and the living were lying as still as the dead. The church clock struck eleven. The air was so empty of other sounds that the whirr of the clockwork immediately before the strokes could be distinctly heard.

Bathsheba's residence was tonight occupied only by Maryann. Liddy was with her sister, whom Bathsheba had set out to visit. A few minutes after eleven had struck, Maryann turned in her bed with a sense of being disturbed. This led to a dream, and the dream to an awakening, with an uneasy sensation that something had happened. She left her bed and looked out of the window. The horse paddock sat adjacent to this end of the building. In the paddock, she could barely make out a figure approaching the horse that was feeding there. The figure seized the horse by the forelock and led it to the corner of the field. In the gray light, Maryann watched as the figure harnessed the horse to a carriage. The next sound she heard was that of a horse trotting down the road, mingled with the sound of light wheels.

Two varieties only of humanity could have entered the paddock with the ghostlike glide of that mysterious figure. They were a woman and a gypsy man. A woman was out of the question at this hour. Therefore, the intruder could be no other than a thief. This suspicion was fueled by the presence of gypsies in Weatherbury Bottom.

Maryann ran to Coggan's, the nearest house, and raised an alarm. Coggan called Gabriel, and together they went to the paddock. Beyond all doubt the horse was gone.

"Listen!" said Gabriel.

They listened. The still air allowed them to hear the sounds of a trotting horse passing up Longpuddle Lane—just beyond the gypsies encampment in Weatherbury Bottom.

"That's our horse Dainty—I'll swear to her step," said Jan.

"We must ride after her," said Gabriel, decisively. "I'll be responsible to Miss Everdene for what we do. Yes, we'll follow."

Oak brought up two horses. "Maryann, you go to bed," Gabriel said. The men mounted their steeds and galloped off in the direction taken by Bathsheba's horse and the robber. Whose vehicle the horse had been harnessed to was a matter of some uncertainty.

Weatherbury Bottom was reached in three or four minutes. They scanned the shady green patch by the roadside. The gypsies were gone.

"The villains!" said Gabriel. "Which way have they gone, I wonder?"

"Straight on, as sure as God made little apples," said Jan.

"Very well. We are better mounted and can overtake them," said Oak. "Now on at full speed!"

They could no longer hear the sound of the horse and vehicle. The road grew softer and more clayey as Weatherbury was left behind, and the late rain had wetted its surface. They came to a crossroads. Coggan suddenly pulled up his horse and slipped off.

"What's the matter?" said Gabriel.

"We must try to track 'em, since we can't hear 'em," said Jan, fumbling in his pockets. He struck a light, and held the match to the ground. The rain had been heavier here, and all foot and horse tracks made previous to the storm had been blurred. One set of tracks was fresh and had no water in them.

"Straight on!" Jan exclaimed. "Tracks like that mean a stiff gallop. No wonder we don't hear him."

"How do you know?"

"Old Jimmy Harris only shoed her last week, and I'd swear to his make among ten thousand."

"The rest of the gypsies must have gone on earlier, or some other way," said Oak. "You saw there were no other tracks?"

"True." They rode along silently for a long, weary time. Coggan carried an old pistol.

They rode and listened. No sound was heard except a creek trickling over rocks. Gabriel dismounted when they came to a turning. Coggan struck another match. This time only three hoofprints were of the regular horseshoe shape. Every fourth was a dot.

"Lame," said Oak.

"Yes. Dainty is lamed; the near-foot-afore," said Coggan slowly, staring still at the footprints.

"We'll push on," said Gabriel, remounting. This last turning took them onto the main road to the large city of Bath.

Before long they spied in the distance the white turnpike gate that crossed the road. Someone was calling for the sleepy-eyed toll-keeper to receive the toll and open the gate.

The keeper came out half-dressed, with a candle in his hand. The rays illumined the whole group.

"Keep the gate closed!" shouted Gabriel. "He has stolen the horse!"

"Who?" said the turnpike-man.

Gabriel looked at the driver of the gig, and saw a woman—Bathsheba!

"Well, Gabriel," she inquired quietly, "where are you going?"

"We thought—" began Gabriel.

"I am driving to Bath," she said. "An important matter made it necessary for me to give up my visit to Liddy, and go off at once. Were you following me?"

"We thought the horse was stolen."

"Well—what a thing! How very foolish of you not to know that I had taken the carriage and horse. I could neither wake Maryann nor get into the house, though I hammered for ten minutes against her windowsill. Fortunately, I could get the key of the coach-house, so I troubled no one further. Didn't you think it might be me?"

"Why should we, Miss?"

"What! Mustn't a lady move an inch from her door without being dogged like a thief?"

"But how was we to know, if you left no account

of your doings?" said Coggan. "And ladies don't drive at these hours, Miss."

"I did leave an account—and you would have seen it in the morning. I wrote in chalk on the coach-house doors that I had come back for the horse and gig, and driven off; that I could arouse nobody, and should return soon."

"But you'll consider, Ma'am, that we couldn't see that till it got daylight."

"True," she said. Though vexed at first, she had too much sense to blame them long or seriously for a devotion to her that was as valuable as it was rare. She added with a very pretty grace, "Well, I really thank you heartily for taking all this trouble."

"Dainty is lame, Miss," said Coggan. "Can ye go on?"

"It was only a stone in her shoe. I got down and pulled it out a hundred yards back. I can manage very well, thank you. I shall be in Bath by daylight. Will you now return, please?"

She turned her head, passed through the gate, and was soon gone. Coggan and Gabriel turned their horses around. Fanned by the velvety air of this July night, they retraced the road by which they had come.

"A strange adventure, this of hers, isn't it, Oak?" said Coggan, curiously.

"Yes," said Gabriel, shortly.

"She won't be in Bath by no daylight!"

"Coggan, suppose we keep this night's work as quiet as we can?"

"I am of one and the same mind."

"Very well. We shall be home by three o'clock or so, and can creep into the parish like lambs."

● ● ●

After her tumultuous meeting with Boldwood, Bathsheba remained greatly perturbed. She eventually concluded that there were only two remedies for the present desperate state of affairs. The first was merely to keep Troy away from Weatherbury till Boldwood's indignation had cooled. The second was to give up Troy altogether. Oh, if only Troy had been Boldwood, and the path of love the sensible one to take.

At last she resolved to see Troy at once. She would implore him to assist her in this dilemma. A letter to keep him away could not reach him in time, even if he should be disposed to listen to it.

Was Bathsheba altogether blind to the obvious fact that the support of a lover's arms is not the best way to strengthen a resolve to give him up? Or was she aware, with a thrill of pleasure, that by adopting this method of getting rid of him, she was ensuring a meeting with him, at any rate, once more?

It was now dark. The only way to accomplish her purpose was to give up her idea of visiting Liddy at Yalbury, return to Weatherbury Farm, attach the horse to the gig, and drive at once to Bath. The scheme seemed at first impossible. The journey was long and difficult, especially for a woman, at night, and alone.

Bathsheba walked slowly. She did not want to enter Weatherbury till the cottagers were in bed, and, particularly, till Boldwood was secure. Her plan was now to drive to Bath during the night. She would see Sergeant Troy in the morning before he set out to come to her. Bathsheba would bid him a final farewell. Early the next morning, she would set out for Liddy at Yalbury. They would then come home to Weatherbury whenever they chose. Nobody would know she had been to Bath at all. Such was Bathsheba's scheme. But, being new to the region, she thought the distance of her journey was only half of what it really was.

This plan she proceeded to carry out, with what initial success we have already seen.

CHAPTER 33

A week passed, and there was no news of Bathsheba.

Then a note came for Maryann. It said that the business which had called her mistress to Bath still detained her there.

Another week passed; still no Bathsheba. The oat-harvest began, and all the men were a-field on a hot July day. Indoors nothing was to be heard save the droning of bluebottle flies. Out of doors, the only sounds were the hissing of scythes as they cut down the oats. Perspiration rained from the foreheads and cheeks of the harvesters. Drought was everywhere.

The men were about to take a break, when Coggan saw a figure in a blue coat and brass buttons running to them across the field.

"I wonder who that is?" he said.

"I hope nothing is wrong about mistress," said Maryann. "An unlucky token came to me indoors this morning. I went to unlock the door and dropped the key. It fell upon the stone floor and broke into two pieces. Breaking a key is a dreadful sign. I wish the mistress was home."

"'Tis Cain Ball," said Gabriel, pausing from sharpening his scythe.

By this time Cainy was nearing the group of harvesters. He was carrying a large slice of bread and ham in one hand, from which he took mouthfuls as he ran. The other hand was wrapped in a bandage. When he came close, he began to cough violently: "Hok-hok-hok!"

At length he blurted out, "I've been visiting to Bath because I had a sore on my thumb; yes, and I've seen— hok, hok!"

As soon as Cain mentioned Bath, they all threw down their scythes and drew round him. Unfortunately, the erratic crumb that lodged in his throat did not improve his narrative powers.

"Yes," he continued, "I've seed the world at last—yes—and I've seed our mis'ess!"

"Well, at Bath you saw—" prompted Gabriel.

"I saw our mistress," continued the junior shepherd, "and a soldier, walking along. They were arm-in-arm, like a courting couple." The coughing resumed. "A fly just—hok, hok—flew down my throat. Well, I see our mis'ess and a sojer—a-hok!"

"Damn the boy!" said Gabriel.

"Here's some cider for him—that'll cure his throat," said Jan Coggan, lifting a flask of cider, pulling out the cork, and draining some into Cainy's mouth.

"Now then," said Gabriel, impatiently, "what did you see, Cain?"

"I seed our mis'ess go into a park, where there's seats, and shrubs and flowers, arm-in-arm with a sojer," continued Cainy. "And I think the sojer was Sergeant Troy. And they sat there together for more than half-an-hour. And she once was crying a'most to death. And when they came out her eyes were shining and she was as white as a lily. And they looked into one another's faces, as love-struck as a man and woman can be."

Following this report, the reapers resumed their work. Gabriel did nothing to show that he was troubled. However, Coggan knew him well, and when they were alone, said, "Don't take on about her, Gabriel. What difference does it make whose sweetheart she is, since she can't be yours?"

"That's the very thing I say to myself," said Gabriel.

CHAPTER 34

That same evening, at dusk, Bathsheba and Liddy returned to the farm.

Boldwood likewise made his way to the farm. He had not been outside his garden since his meeting with Bathsheba. It had taken time, but he had now come to his senses and wanted to apologize and beg forgiveness of Bathsheba for his violent behavior. He had just heard of Bathsheba's return—only from a visit to Liddy, as he supposed. He was unaware of her stay in Bath.

Boldwood knocked on the front door of Bathsheba's house and inquired for Miss Everdene. Liddy's manner was odd, but he did not notice it. She went in, leaving him standing in the doorway.

After a moment, Liddy came out. "My mistress cannot see you, sir," she said.

The farmer instantly went out by the gate. He was unforgiven—that was the meaning of it all.

Boldwood did not hurry homeward. It was at least ten o'clock when, walking deliberately through the lower part of Weatherbury, he heard a carriage entering the village. The van ran a regular route to and from a town in a northern direction, and it was owned and driven by a Weatherbury man. The carriage pulled up to this man's house. The lamp fixed to the hood illuminated a scarlet and gilded form, who was the first to get out.

"Ah!" said Boldwood to himself, "come to see her again."

Troy entered the driver's house, which had been the place of his lodging on his last visit to his native town. Ten minutes later, Troy emerged from the house, carrying a small suitcase. Boldwood hastened up to him.

"Sergeant Troy?"

"Yes—I'm Sergeant Troy."

"Just arrived from up the country, I think?"

"Just arrived from Bath."

"I am William Boldwood."

"Indeed."

"I wish to speak a word with you," he said.

"What about?"

"About her who lives just ahead there—and about another woman you have wronged."

"I wonder at your impertinence," said Troy, moving on. Then he heard the determination in Boldwood's voice and saw that Boldwood was carrying a thick stick.

"Very well, I'll listen with pleasure," said Troy, placing his bag on the ground. "Only speak low, for somebody may overhear us in the farmhouse there."

Boldwood said, "I know a good deal concerning Fanny Robin's attachment to you. I may say, too, that I believe I am the only person in the village, excepting Gabriel Oak, who does know it. You ought to marry her."

"I suppose I ought. Indeed, I wish to, but I cannot."

"Why?"

Troy was about to utter something hastily. He then stopped himself and said, "I am too poor." His voice had changed. Previously it had had a careless tone. It was the voice of a trickster now.

Boldwood continued, "I may as well speak plainly. I don't wish to express any opinion on your conduct. I intend a business transaction with you."

"I see," said Troy. "Suppose we sit down here."

An old tree trunk lay under the hedge immediately opposite, and they sat down.

"I was engaged to be married to Miss Everdene," said Boldwood, "but you came and—"

"Not engaged," said Troy.

"As good as engaged. If you had not come I should certainly—yes, CERTAINLY—have been accepted by this time. If you had not seen her, you might have been married to Fanny. Well, there's too much difference between Miss Everdene's station and your own for this flirtation with her ever to result in marriage. So all I ask is, don't pay her attention any more. Marry Fanny. I'll make it worth your while."

"How will you?"

"I'll pay you well now. I'll settle a sum of money upon Fanny. And I'll see that you don't suffer from poverty in the future. I'll put it clearly. Bathsheba is only playing with you. You are too poor for her, as I said. Give up wasting your time about a great match you'll never make for a moderate and rightful match you may make tomorrow. Leave Weatherbury now, this night, and you shall take fifty pounds with you. Fanny shall have fifty to enable her to prepare for the wedding. She shall have five hundred more on her wedding-day."

"I do like Fanny best," said Troy. "And if, as you say, Miss Everdene is out of my reach, I have all to gain by accepting your money and marrying Fan. But she's only a servant."

"Never mind—do you agree to my arrangement?"

"I do."

"Ah!" said Boldwood. "Oh, Troy, if you like her best, why then did you step in here and injure my happiness?"

"I love Fanny best now," said Troy. "But Bathsh—Miss Everdene inflamed me, and displaced Fanny for a time. It is over now."

"Then why did you come here again to see her?"

"There are weighty reasons. Fifty pounds at once, you said!"

"I did," said Boldwood, "and here they are— fifty sovereigns." He handed Troy a small packet.

"Stop, listen!" said Troy in a whisper.

A light pit-pat was heard upon the road just above them.

"By George—'tis she," he continued. "I must go on and meet her."

"She—who?"

"Bathsheba."

"Bathsheba—out alone at this time o' night!" said Boldwood in amazement, and starting up. "Why must you meet her?"

"She was expecting me tonight—and I must now speak to her, and wish her good-bye, according to your wish."

"I don't see the necessity of speaking."

"It can do no harm—and she'll be wandering about looking for me if I don't. You shall hear all I say to her. Now sit still there, hold my suitcase, and pay attention to what you hear."

The light footstep came closer, halting occasionally, as if the walker listened for a sound. Troy whistled a double note in a soft, fluty tone.

Troy stepped forward.

"Frank, dearest, is that you?" The tones were Bathsheba's.

"Yes," said Troy to her.

"How late you are," she continued, tenderly. "Did you come by the coach? I heard its wheels entering the village, but it was some time ago. I had almost given you up, Frank."

"I was sure to come," said Frank. "You knew I should, did you not?"

"Well, I thought you would," she said, playfully. "And, Frank, we are so lucky! There's not a soul in my house but me tonight. I've packed them all off so nobody on earth will know of your visit to your lady's bedroom. Liddy went to her grandfather's to tell him about her holiday."

"Wonderful," said Troy. "But I had better go back for my suitcase, because my slippers and brush and comb are in it. You run home while I fetch it. I promise to be with you in ten minutes."

"Yes." She turned and tripped up the hill again.

This dialogue produced a nervous twitching of Boldwood's tightly closed lips, and his face became bathed in a clammy dew. He now started forward toward Troy. Troy turned to him and took up the suitcase.

"Shall I tell her I have come to give her up and cannot marry her?" said the soldier, mockingly.

"No, no; wait a minute. I want to say more to you!" said Boldwood, in a hoarse whisper.

"Now," said Troy, "you see my dilemma. Perhaps I am a bad man—the victim of my impulses. I can't, however, marry them both. And I have two reasons for choosing Fanny. First, I like her best. Second, you make it worth my while."

At the same instant Boldwood sprang upon him, and held him by the neck. Troy felt Boldwood's grasp slowly tightening.

"A moment," he gasped.

Boldwood loosened his hand, saying, "By Heaven, I've a mind to kill you!"

"And ruin Bathsheba."

"Save her."

"Oh, how can her honor be preserved now, unless I marry her?"

Boldwood groaned. He reluctantly released the soldier, and flung him back against the hedge. "Devil, you torture me!" said he.

Troy rebounded like a ball, and was about to make a dash at the farmer; but he checked himself,

saying lightly, "It is not worth my while to fight you. Indeed, it is a barbarous way of settling a quarrel. I shall shortly leave the army because of the same conviction. Now that you have seen how matters stand with Bathsheba, 'twould be a mistake to kill me, would it not?"

"'Twould be a mistake to kill you," repeated Boldwood, mechanically, with a bowed head.

"Better kill yourself."

"Far better."

"I'm glad you see it."

"Troy, make her your wife, and don't act upon what I arranged just now. The alternative is dreadful, but take Bathsheba. I give her up! She must love you indeed to sell soul and body to you so utterly as she has done."

"But about Fanny?"

"Bathsheba is a well-to-do woman," continued Boldwood. "She will make a good wife."

"But she has a will—not to say a temper, and I shall be a mere slave to her. I could do anything with poor Fanny Robin."

"Troy," said Boldwood, imploringly, "I'll do anything for you, only don't desert her. Please don't desert her, Troy."

"Which, poor Fanny?"

"No. Bathsheba Everdene. Love her best! Love her tenderly! How shall I get you to see how advantageous it will be to you to secure her at once?"

"I don't wish to secure her in any new way."

Boldwood made ready to strike Troy again, but he checked his impulse.

Troy went on, "I shall soon purchase my discharge, and then—"

"But for Bathsheba's honor, I wish you to hasten on this marriage! You love each other, and you must let me help you to do it."

"How?"

"Why, by settling the five hundred on Bathsheba instead of Fanny, to enable you to marry at once. No. She wouldn't accept it from me now. I'll pay it to you on the wedding-day."

Troy said, "And am I to have anything now?"

"Yes, if you wish to. But I have not much additional money with me. I did not expect this. But all I have is yours."

Boldwood searched his pockets.

"I have twenty-one pounds more with me," he said. "But before I leave you I must have a paper signed—"

"Pay me the money, and we'll go straight to her house and make any arrangement you please. But she must know nothing of this cash business."

"Nothing, nothing," said Boldwood, hastily. "Here is the money. If you'll come to my house, we'll write out the agreement for the remainder."

"First we'll call upon her."

They went up the hill to Bathsheba's house. When they stood at the entrance, Troy said, "Wait here a moment." Opening the door, he glided inside, leaving the door ajar.

Boldwood waited. In two minutes, a light appeared in the passage. Boldwood then saw that the chain had been fastened across the door. Troy appeared inside, carrying a bedroom candlestick.

"What, did you think I should break in?" said Boldwood.

"Oh, no, it is merely my habit to secure things. Will you read this a moment? I'll hold the light."

Troy handed a folded newspaper through the slit between door and doorpost, and put the candle close. "That's the paragraph," he said, placing his finger on a line.

Boldwood looked and read:

MARRIAGES
"On the 17th inst., at St. Ambrose's Church, Bath, by the Rev. G. Mincing, B.A., Francis Troy, only son of the late

Edward Troy, Esq., M.D., of Weatherbury, and sergeant with Dragoon Guards, to Bathsheba, only surviving daughter of the late Mr. John Everdene, of Casterbridge.

The paper fell from Boldwood's hands.

Troy continued, "Fifty pounds to marry Fanny. Good. Twenty-one pounds not to marry Fanny, but Bathsheba. Good. Finale: already Bathsheba's husband. Now, Boldwood, yours is the ridiculous fate which always comes from interfering between a man and his wife. And another word. Bad as I am, I am not such a rogue as to put up any marriage for sale. Fanny has long ago left me. I don't know where she is. I have searched everywhere. Now that I've taught you a lesson, take your money back again."

"I will not. I will not!" said Boldwood, in a hiss.

"Anyhow I won't have it," said Troy, contemptuously. He threw the money into the road.

Boldwood shook his clenched fist at him. "You villain of Satan! You filthy hound! But I'll punish you yet. Mark me, I'll punish you yet!"

Another peal of laughter. Troy then closed the door and locked himself in.

Throughout the whole of that night, Boldwood's dark form might have been seen walking about the hills and downs of Weatherbury, like an unhappy ghost in the land of the dead.

CHAPTER 35

It was very early the next morning—a time of sun and dew. Just before the clock struck five, Gabriel Oak and Coggan went on together to the fields. As they passed near their mistress's house, they saw an upper window being opened. A handsome man lazily leaned out and looked from side to side. The man was Sergeant Troy. His red jacket was loosely thrown on, but not buttoned. He appeared to be very much at home.

Coggan spoke first, looking quietly at the window. "She has married him!" he said.

Gabriel made no reply.

"I thought we might hear something today," continued Coggan. He glanced around at Gabriel. "Good heavens above us, Oak, how white your face is. You look like a corpse! Lean on the gate. I'll wait a bit."

"All right, all right."

They stood by the gate awhile, Gabriel listlessly staring at the ground. That they were married he had instantly decided. Why had it been so mysteriously managed? It was not Bathsheba's way to do things secretly. The union was an unutterable grief to him.

In a few minutes, they moved on again toward the house. The sergeant still looked from the window.

"Morning, comrades!" he shouted, in a cheery voice, when they came up.

Coggan replied to the greeting. "Aren't ye going to answer the man?" he then said to Gabriel. "I'd say 'good morning.' You needn't mean it, you know."

Gabriel soon decided that, since the deed was done, to put the best face upon the matter.

"Good morning, Sergeant Troy," he returned, in a ghastly voice.

"Well," said Troy, "I shall be down in the fields with you some time this week. But I have a few matters to attend to first. So good-day to you. We shall, of course, keep on friendly terms as usual. I'm not a proud man: nobody is ever able to say that of Sergeant Troy. However, what is must be, and here's half-a-crown to drink my health, men."

Troy threw the coin over the fence towards Gabriel, who let it fall, his face turning an angry red. Coggan edged forward and picked it up as it lay in the road.

"Very well—you keep it, Coggan," said Gabriel almost fiercely. "As for me, I'll do without gifts from him!"

"Don't show it too much," said Coggan, musingly. "For if he's married to her, mark my words, he'll buy his discharge and be our master here. Therefore 'tis well to say 'Friend' outwardly, though you say 'Trouble' within."

CHAPTER 36

One night late in August, the sky had a menacing aspect. The moon had a strange, metallic look, and the clouds seemed to be jockeying for position. Torrential rains were likely to fall.

Oak gazed with worry at eight uncovered ricks. Each was bursting with the rich produce of the farm for that year. He went on to the barn.

Sergeant Troy was now supervising the farm. He had previously purchased his discharge from the army. This was the night he had selected for giving the harvest supper and dance. As Oak approached the barn, he could hear the sound of fiddles and a tambourine. He came close to the large doors, one of which stood slightly ajar, and looked in.

The central space was cleared away for the feast and dancing. Green foliage decorated the walls. Bathsheba and Troy were seated at a table at one end of the building, surrounded by revelers. When the music and dancing came to a pause, Gabriel entered the building. He avoided Bathsheba, and got as near as possible to where Sergeant Troy was now seated, drinking brandy and water. Gabriel could not get within speaking distance of him, so he sent a message, asking him to come over for a moment. The sergeant told the messenger he could not do so.

"Will you tell him, then," said Gabriel, "that I only wished to say that a heavy rain is sure to fall soon, and that something should be done to protect the ricks?"

"Mr. Troy says it will not rain," returned the messenger, "and he cannot stop to talk to you about such bother."

Before heading home, Oak stopped at the door for one last look. Troy was speaking.

"Friends, it is not only the harvest that we are celebrating tonight. This is also a wedding feast. A short time ago I had the happiness to marry this lady, your mistress. Not until now have we been able to celebrate this event publicly. To celebrate appropriately, I have ordered some bottles of brandy and kettles of hot water. A triple-strength goblet will he handed round to each guest."

Bathsheba put her hand on Troy's arm and, with pale face, begged him, "No—don't give it to them—pray don't, Frank! It will only do them harm. They have had enough of everything."

"Hah!" said the sergeant contemptuously. "We'll send the women-folk home! Then we men can drink to our hearts' content! If any of the men refuse, let them look elsewhere for a winter's work."

Bathsheba indignantly left the barn, followed by all the women and children. Troy and the men on the farm remained behind. Oak, not to appear disagreeable, stayed a little while and then departed.

Feeling uneasy about the weather, Gabriel knew he could trust the instincts of the sheep on the matter. He walked out to the flock. The sheep were crowded close together, something they did only when feeling terror. Furthermore, their tails faced the direction from which the storm threatened. He knew now that he was right, and that Troy was wrong.

Oak returned to the yard where the ricks were stored. There were five wheat-ricks and three stacks of barley. Gabriel estimated their value at 750 pounds, a huge sum. All would be lost unless the ricks were covered to protect them from the approaching rain.

Should the risk be run of destroying the corn, because of the instability of a woman? "Never, if I can prevent it!" said Gabriel. But he was also thinking, "I will help to my last effort the woman I have loved so dearly."

Gabriel returned to the barn to get help. When he looked in, an unusual picture met his eye. The candles, suspended among the evergreens, had burnt down to their bases. All the men-folk lay unconscious at various angles upon the chairs and floor. In the midst of these shone red and distinct the figure of Sergeant Troy, leaning back in a chair.

Gabriel glanced hopelessly at the group. Sergeant Troy had strenuously insisted, glass in hand, that they drink with him, so the men had not refused. But since they were unaccustomed to any liquor stronger than cider or mild ale, it was no wonder that they had succumbed, one and all, after only an hour. He realized at once that if the ricks were to be saved, he must save them with his own hands.

Gabriel went out again into the night. A hot breeze, as if breathed from the parted lips of some dragon about to swallow the globe, fanned him from the south. Directly opposite in the north rose a grim misshapen body of cloud.

Ten minutes later his lonely figure might have been seen dragging four large waterproof coverings across the yard. Soon two of the wheat-ricks were covered snugly—two cloths to each. Since there were no more cloths, Oak did his best to protect the remaining three wheat-stacks by sloping them with his pitchfork. This would save the stacks, if there was not much wind.

Next came the barley. This could be protected only by thatching, covering the grain with woven reeds. Gabriel worked feverishly to accomplish this. Time went on, and the moon vanished. It would not reappear. The night had a haggard look, like a sick thing. Finally there came a slow breeze, like the final exhaled breath of someone dying.

CHAPTER 37

A light flashed over the scene, and a rumble filled the air. It was the first move of the approaching storm. The lightning increased, now silver. It gleamed in the heavens as though it were reflected off a sky-born army of knights in full armor.

The flashes illuminated a herd of cows, galloping about in the wildest and maddest confusion, flinging their heels and tails high into the air.

Not a drop of rain had fallen as yet. Oak wiped his weary brow. Another flash of lightning appeared, with the spring of a serpent and the shout of a fiend. What was this that the light revealed to him? In the open ground before him, as he looked over the ridge of the rick, was a dark and apparently female form. Could it be Bathsheba?

"Is that you, Ma'am?" said Gabriel.

"Who is there?" said the voice of Bathsheba.

"Gabriel. I am on the rick, thatching."

"Oh, Gabriel! The weather awoke me, and I thought of the crop. I am so distressed about it—can we save it? I cannot find my husband. Is he with you?"

"He is not here."

"Do you know where he is?"

"Asleep in the barn."

"He promised that the stacks should be seen to, and now they are all neglected! Can I do anything to help? Surely I can do something?"

"You can bring up some reed-sheaves to me, one by one, Ma'am, if you are not afraid to come up the ladder in the dark," said Gabriel. "Every moment is precious now, and that would save a good deal of time."

"I'll do anything!" Bathsheba said, resolutely. She instantly took a sheaf upon her shoulder, clambered up close to his heels, placed it behind the rod, and descended for another. At her third ascent, lightning flashed; then came the peal of thunder.

"How terrible!" Bathsheba exclaimed, and clutched him by the sleeve. Gabriel turned and steadied her by holding her arm.

The next flare came. Bathsheba was on the ground now, carrying another sheaf, and she bore its dazzle without flinching—thunder and all—and again ascended with the load. There was then a silence everywhere for four or five minutes. Gabriel thought the crisis of the storm had passed. But there came a burst of light.

"Hold on!" said Gabriel, taking the sheaf from her shoulder, and grasping her arm again.

Heaven opened then, indeed. The flash sprang from east, west, north, south, and was a perfect dance of death. The forms of skeletons appeared in the air, shaped with blue fire for bones—dancing, leaping, striding, and mingling in unparalleled confusion. With these were intertwined snakes of green, rising and falling, and behind these was a broad mass of lesser light. From every part of the tumbling sky came a shout. In the meantime one of the grisly forms had alighted upon the point of Gabriel's rod, to run invisibly down it, down the chain, and into the earth. Gabriel was almost blinded, and he could feel Bathsheba's warm arm tremble in his hand—a sensation new and thrilling. But love, life, everything human, seemed small and trifling beside the spectacle of an infuriated universe.

Oak had hardly time to gather up these impressions into a thought, when the tall tree on the hill blazed with a white heat, and a new, louder blast sounded, harsh and pitiless. Oak saw that lightning had struck the tree. It was sliced down the whole length of its tall, straight stem. Half the tree remained erect, and revealed the bared surface as a strip of white down the front. A sulfurous smell filled the air; then all was dark and silent.

"We had a narrow escape!" said Gabriel, hurriedly. "You had better go down."

Bathsheba said nothing; but he could distinctly hear her frightened breathing. She descended the ladder, and he followed. They both stood still at the bottom, side by side. Bathsheba appeared to think only of the weather—Oak thought only of her. At last he said, "The storm seems to have passed now, at any rate."

"I think so too," said Bathsheba. "Though there are multitudes of gleams, look!"

"Nothing serious," said he. "I cannot understand no rain falling. But Heaven be praised, it is all the better for us. I am now going up again."

"Gabriel, you are kinder than I deserve," Bathsheba said. "Oh, why are not some of the others here!"

"They would have been here if they could," said Oak, in a hesitating way.

"Oh, I know it all—all," she said, adding slowly, "They are all asleep in the barn, in a drunken sleep, and my husband among them."

After a pause, Bathsheba went on.

"Gabriel, I suppose you thought that when I galloped away to Bath that night it was on purpose to be married?"

"I did," he answered.

"And others thought so, too?"

"Yes."

"And you blamed me for it?"

"Well—a little."

"I thought so. Now, I care a little for your good opinion, and I want to explain something. I went to Bath that night with the intention of breaking off my engagement to Mr. Troy. It was owing to circumstances which occurred after I got there that—that we were married. Now, do you see the matter in a new light?"

"I do—somewhat."

"I must, I suppose, say more, now that I have begun. And perhaps it's no harm, for you are certainly under no delusion that I ever loved you. Well, I was alone in a strange city, and the horse was lame. I didn't know what to do. I was coming away, when he suddenly appeared. He said that he had that day seen a woman more beautiful than me.

He said too that unless I married him at once, he could not guarantee that we would be married ever. I was greatly troubled." She cleared her voice, and waited a moment, as if to gather breath. "And then, between jealousy and distraction, I married him!" she whispered.

Gabriel made no reply.

"And now I don't wish for a single remark from you upon the subject—indeed, I forbid it. I only wanted you to know that misunderstood bit of my history."

They continued to work. Oak could see that Bathsheba was moving more slowly now. He said to her, gently, "I think you had better go indoors now. You are tired. I can finish the rest alone. If the wind does not change, the rain is likely to keep off."

"Thank you for your devotion, a thousand times, Gabriel! Goodnight—I know you are doing your very best for me."

Bathsheba walked away in the darkness. Oak heard the latch of the gate fall as she passed through. He fell into a thoughtful reverie. He was disturbed in his meditation by a grating noise from the coach-house. It was the vane on the roof turning round. This change in the wind was the signal for a disastrous rain.

CHAPTER 38

It was now five o'clock in the morning. Cool breezes blew round Oak's face, as he slaved away again at the barley. A huge drop of rain struck his face, and the trees rocked to the bases of their trunks. The rain came on in earnest, and Oak soon felt the water digging cold and clammy routes down his back.

Oak suddenly remembered that eight months before this time, he had been fighting against fire in the same spot as desperately as he was fighting against water now—and because of a futile love for the same woman.

It was about seven o'clock in the dark leaden morning when Gabriel came down from the last stack, and thankfully exclaimed, "It is done!" He was drenched and weary.

Faint sounds came from the barn, and he looked that way. Figures stepped singly and in pairs through the doors. All stumbled awkwardly, except for the foremost, who wore a red jacket, and advanced with his hands in his pockets, whistling. Not a single one of them looked toward the ricks or seemed to give them a single thought.

Oak too headed for home. On the way, he

saw a person walking yet more slowly than himself under an umbrella. The man was Boldwood.

"How are you this morning, sir?" said Oak.

"Yes, it is a wet day. Oh, I am well, very well, I thank you."

"I am glad to hear it, sir. I've been working hard to get our ricks covered, and was barely in time. Yours of course are safe, sir."

"No. I overlooked the ricks this year."

"Then not a tenth of your grain will be in condition for sale, sir," Oak exclaimed in shocked amazement.

"Possibly not."

It is difficult to describe the intensely dramatic effect that announcement had upon Oak at such a moment. A few months earlier Boldwood's neglecting this task would have been as unthinkable an idea as a sailor forgetting he was on a ship. Oak was thinking that whatever he himself might have suffered from Bathsheba's marriage, here was a man who had suffered more.

Boldwood's voice changed as he switched to a new topic. "Oak, you know as well as I that things have gone wrong with me lately."

"I thought the woman I work for would have married you," said Gabriel. "However, nothing happens that we expect," he added.

"I suppose I am a joke about the parish," said Boldwood.

"Oh no—I don't think that."

"—But the real truth of the matter is that there was not, as some think, any jilting on her part. No engagement ever existed between me and Miss Everdene. She never promised me!" Boldwood stood still now and turned his wild face to Oak. "Oh, Gabriel," he continued, "I am weak and foolish, and I can't cast off my miserable grief! I had some faint belief in the mercy of God till I lost that woman. Now I feel it is better to die than to live!"

In a moment, Boldwood recovered, and when he next spoke, it was with his usual reserve. "I do feel a little regret occasionally, but no woman ever had power over me for any length of time. Well, good morning. I can trust you not to mention to others what has passed between us two here."

CHAPTER 39

On the turnpike road, between Casterbridge and Weatherbury, is Yalbury Hill. This is one of those steep inclines which pervade the highways of this hilly region. In returning from market, it is usual for the travelers to step out of their wagons and walk up.

One Saturday evening in the month of October, Bathsheba's vehicle was duly creeping up this incline. She was sitting listlessly in the gig. Her husband Troy walked beside. Though on foot, he held the reins and whip, and occasionally aimed harmless cuts at the horse's ear with the whip.

"Yes, if it hadn't been for that wretched rain, I should have won two hundred pounds, my love," he was saying. "Don't you see, the rain altered all the odds?"

"But the weather is changeable this time of year."

"Well, yes. The fact is, these autumn horseraces are the ruin of everybody. Never did I see such a day as 'twas! The race course is in a wild open place, just out of Budmouth. A drab sea rolled in toward us like liquid misery. Wind and rain—good Lord!"

"What you mean to say, Frank," said Bathsheba, sadly, "is that you have lost more than a hundred pounds in a month by this dreadful horseracing. Oh, Frank, it is cruel and foolish of you to spend my money so. We shall have to sell the farm if you keep up with this."

"Nonsense," was his reply. Then, seeing that she was nearly in tears, "Now, there 'tis again—turn on the waterworks; that's just like you."

"But you'll promise me not to go to Budmouth for the next race, won't you?" she implored.

"I don't see why I should. In fact, if it turns out to be a fine day, I was thinking of taking you."

"Never, never! I'll go a hundred miles the other way first!"

"But you don't have to go to the race in order to bet, my love. The bets are made well before the race begins."

"But you don't mean to say that you have risked anything on this one too!" she exclaimed, with an agonized look.

"There now, don't you be a little fool. Wait till you are told. Why, Bathsheba, you have lost all the pluck and sauciness you formerly had. If I had known what a chicken-hearted creature you were under all your boldness, I'd never have—I know what."

A flash of indignation flared in Bathsheba's dark eyes. She looked resolutely ahead, and they moved on without further speech.

A woman appeared on the crest of the hill, walking toward them. While the oncoming night shrouded the woman's face, Bathsheba could see the extreme poverty of her clothes.

"Please, sir, do you know at what time Casterbridge Union House closes at night?" the woman said to Troy.

Troy started visibly at the sound of the voice, then quickly regained his composure. He said, slowly, "I don't know."

The woman, on hearing him speak, looked up and recognized the soldier under the gentleman-farmer's garb. She uttered a hysterical cry and fell down.

"Oh, poor thing!" exclaimed Bathsheba, instantly preparing to come down from the wagon to lend assistance.

"Stay where you are, and attend to the horse!" ordered Troy, throwing her the reins and the whip. "Walk the horse to the top. I'll see to the woman."

The horse, gig, and Bathsheba moved on.

"How on earth did you come here? I thought you were miles away, or dead! Why didn't you write to me?" said Troy to the woman, in a strangely gentle, yet hurried voice, as he lifted her up.

"I feared to."

"Have you any money?"

"None."

"Good Heaven—I wish I had more to give you! Here's every coin I have left. I have none but what my wife gives me, you know, and I can't ask her now."

The woman made no answer.

"I have only another moment," continued Troy; "and now listen. Where are you going tonight? Casterbridge Union?"

"Yes. I thought to go there."

"You shan't go to that poorhouse. Yet wait. Yes, perhaps for tonight. Sleep there tonight and stay there tomorrow. Monday is the first free day I have. On Monday morning, at ten exactly, meet me on Grey's Bridge just out of the town. I'll bring all the money I can gather. You shan't stay poor, Fanny. Then I'll get you a place to stay somewhere. Good-bye till then. I am a brute—but good-bye!"

Troy then rejoined his wife, took the reins from her hand, and whipped the horse into a trot. He was rather agitated.

"Do you know who that woman was?" said Bathsheba, looking searchingly into his face.

"I do," he said, looking boldly back into hers.

"I thought you did," said she, in angry and frosty tones. "Who is she?"

"Nothing to either of us," he said. "I know her by sight."

"What is her name?"

"How should I know her name?"

"I think you do."

"Think what you will, and be—" The sentence was ended by a sharp cut of the whip on the horse's flank. No more was said.

CHAPTER 40

For a considerable time the woman walked on. Her steps became feebler. She strained her eyes to look ahead down the road, now indistinct among the shadows of night. At length her walk dwindled to the merest totter, and she opened a gate, within which was a haystack. Underneath this she sat down and presently slept.

When the woman awoke, it was to find herself surrounded by a moonless and starless night. A distant glow hung over the town of Casterbridge. Toward this weak, soft glow the woman turned her eyes.

"If I could only get there!" she said. "Meet him the day after tomorrow. God help me! Perhaps I shall be in my grave before then."

The woman shuffled on. Presently there became visible a dim white shape. It was another milestone.

"Two more miles!" she said in a hoarse whisper.

She rested against the stone for a short interval, then bestirred herself, and trudged on. At length, she came upon heaps of white chips strewn upon the ground. Woodmen had been working here during the day. Rummaging around, the woman came across two sticks. These sticks were nearly straight to the height of three or four feet, where each branched into a fork like the letter Y. She placed one of these forks under each arm as a crutch, and swung herself forward.

The crutches helped for a time. But soon she was exhausted, and each swing forward became fainter. At last she swayed sideways, and fell.

Here she lay, a shapeless heap, for ten minutes. Then the woman desperately turned round upon her knees and rose to her feet. Onward she struggled, passing yet another milestone. The Casterbridge lights were now individually visible.

After a few more steps, the woman fell exhausted. Hopelessness had come at last.

"No further!" she whispered, and closed her eyes.

Drifting in and out of consciousness, she became aware of something touching her hand. It was soft and warm. She opened her eyes and beheld a dog, which was licking her cheek.

He was a huge, heavy, and quiet creature, standing darkly against the low horizon, and of indeterminate breed. The animal, who was as homeless as she, respectfully withdrew a step or two when the woman moved. Seeing that she did not repulse him, he licked her hand again.

A thought occurred to her. "Perhaps I can make use of him. I might get there yet."

She pointed in the direction of Casterbridge. The dog took a few steps in that direction. Then, finding she could not follow, he came back and whined.

The woman rose to a stooping posture and rested her two little arms upon the shoulders of the dog. She murmured a few stimulating words, and her new friend moved forward slowly. She found herself able to take small mincing steps while placing half her weight upon the animal. Their progress was necessarily very slow. In this manner they passed through the town and reached the Union House.

This stone building consisted of a central structure and two wings. Ivy covered much of the walls, as if nature sought to hide the grim lives of the poor folks within. By the front door hung a bellpull made of a hanging wire. The woman raised herself as high as possible upon her knees, and could just reach the handle. She moved it and fell forward.

A man appeared, discovered the panting heap of clothes, and went back for assistance. With the help of two women, he lifted the collapsed figure and brought her in.

"There is a dog outside," murmured the overcome traveler. "Where is he gone? He helped me."

"I stoned him away," said the man.

Thus they entered the house and disappeared.

CHAPTER 41

Bathsheba said very little to her husband the evening of their return from market. He had little to say to her. The next day, which was Sunday, passed nearly in the same manner. This was the day before the Budmouth races. In the evening Troy said, suddenly, "Bathsheba, could you let me have twenty pounds?"

Her countenance instantly sank. "Twenty pounds?" she said.

"The fact is, I want it badly." The anxiety upon Troy's face was unusual and very marked.

"Ah! for those races tomorrow."

Troy made no reply. Bathsheba's mistaken assumption might serve him well. "Well, suppose I do want it for races?" he said, at last.

"Oh, Frank!" Bathsheba replied. "Only a few weeks ago you said that I was far sweeter than all your other pleasures put together, and that you would give them all up for me. Won't you give up this one? Say yes to your wife—say yes!"

Had the woman not been his wife, Troy would have yielded instantly. As it was, he thought he would not deceive her longer. "The money is not wanted for racing debts at all," he said.

"What is it for?" she asked.

"You wrong me by asking such probing questions," he said. "Bathsheba, don't go too far, or you may have cause to regret something."

She reddened. "I do that already," she said, quickly.

"What do you regret?"

"That my romance has come to an end."

"All romances end at marriage."

"I wish you wouldn't talk like that."

"Come, Bathsheba, let's call a truce with the twenty pounds, and be friends."

She gave a sigh of resignation. "I have about that sum here for household expenses. If you must have it, take it."

"Very good. Thank you. I expect I shall be out by the time you appear for breakfast tomorrow."

"Must you go? There was a time, Frank, when it would have taken a team of wild horses to drag you away from me. You used to call me darling, then. But it doesn't matter to you how my days are passed now."

"I must go, although I'd rather not." As he spoke, Troy glanced idly at his pocket watch. He opened the case at the back, revealing a small coil of hair.

Bathsheba saw the hair. She flushed in pain and surprise. "A woman's curl of hair!" she said. "Oh, Frank, whose is that?"

Troy had instantly closed his watch. He carelessly replied, "Why, yours, of course. Whose should it be? I had quite forgotten that I had it."

"What a dreadful lie, Frank! It was yellow hair."

"Nonsense."

"That's insulting me. I know it was yellow. Now whose was it? I want to know."

"Very well—I'll tell you. It is the hair of a young woman I was going to marry before I knew you."

"You ought to tell me her name, then."

"I cannot do that."

"Is she married yet?"

"No."

"Is she alive?"

"Yes."

"Is she pretty?"

"Yes. Bathsheba, don't be so jealous. You knew what married life would be like. You shouldn't have married if you feared these situations."

Bathsheba let all her bitterness come out. "This is all I get for loving you so well! Ah! when I married you, your life was dearer to me than my own. I would have died for you! Well, you shouldn't keep people's hair. You'll burn it, won't you, Frank?"

Frank went on as if he had not heard her. "There are matters I must take care of, ties you know nothing about. If you regret marrying, so do I."

Trembling now, she put her hand upon his arm and said, "I only regret it if you love another woman more than me. You don't regret it because you already love somebody better than you love me, don't you?"

"I don't know. Why do you say that?"

"You won't burn that curl. You like the woman who owns that pretty hair. Does it belong to the woman we met on the road?"

"Yes. There, now that you have wormed it out of me, I hope you are content."

"And what ties do you have with her?"

"Oh! That meant nothing—a mere jest."

"A mere jest!" she said, in mournful astonishment. "Can you jest when I am so wretchedly in earnest? Tell me the truth, Frank. I don't want much; bare justice—that's all! Ah! once I felt I could be content with nothing less than the highest devotion from the husband I should choose. Now, anything short of cruelty will content me. Yes! the independent and spirited Bathsheba is come to this!"

"For Heaven's sake, don't be so hysterical!" Troy snapped and walked out of the room.

As soon as he had gone, Bathsheba burst into great sobs. But she determined to repress all evidences of feeling. She was conquered, but she would never admit it as long as she lived. She chafed to and fro in rebelliousness, like a caged leopard. Her whole soul was in arms, and the blood fired her face. Until she had met Troy, Bathsheba had been proud of her position as a woman. It had been a glory to her to know that her lips had been touched by no man's on earth—that her waist had never been encircled by a lover's arm. She hated herself now. In those earlier days she had always nourished a secret contempt for girls who were the slaves of the first good-looking young fellow who should choose to salute them. That she had never, by look, word, or sign, encouraged a man to approach her—that she had felt herself sufficient to herself, were facts now bitterly remembered.

The next morning she rose earlier than usual, and had the horse saddled for her ride round the farm in the customary way. When she came in at half-past eight—their usual hour for breakfasting— she was informed that her husband had risen, taken his breakfast, and driven off to Casterbridge.

After breakfast she was cool and collected— quite herself in fact—and she strolled to the gate, intending to walk to another quarter of the farm. As she reached it, she saw Boldwood coming up the road. The farmer stopped when still a long way off, and held up his hand to Gabriel Oak, who was in a footpath across the field. The two men then approached each other and seemed to engage in earnest conversation.

Thus they continued for a long time. Joseph Poorgrass now passed near them, wheeling a barrow of apples up the hill to Bathsheba's residence. Boldwood and Gabriel called to him and spoke to him for a few minutes. Then all three parted. Joseph came up the hill with his barrow. Bathsheba asked him what all the talk was about.

"You'll never see Fanny Robin no more, Ma'am," said the workman.

"Why?"

"Because she's dead in the Union House."

"Fanny—dead—never!"

"Yes, Ma'am."

"What did she die from?"

"I don't know for certain. She was took bad in the morning and, being quite feeble and worn out, she died in the evening. She belongs by law to our parish. Mr. Boldwood is going to send a wagon at three this afternoon to fetch her home here and bury her."

"Indeed I shall not let Mr. Boldwood do any such thing. I shall do it! Fanny was my uncle's servant. Although I only knew her for a couple of days, she belongs to me. How very, very sad this is—the idea of Fanny being in a workhouse!" Bathsheba had begun to know what suffering was, and she spoke with real feeling. "Send word to Mr. Boldwood that Mrs. Troy will take upon herself the duty of fetching an old servant of the family. Joseph, use the new spring wagon with the blue body and red wheels, and wash it very clean. And, Joseph—"

"Yes, Ma'am."

"Carry with you some evergreens and flowers to put upon her coffin—indeed, gather a great many, and completely bury her in them. And let old Pleasant pull the wagon, because she knew him so well."

"I will, Ma'am."

"Dear me—Casterbridge Union—and is Fanny come to this?" said Bathsheba. "I wish I had known of it sooner. I thought she was far away. How long has she lived there?"

"On'y been there a day or two."

"Oh! Then she has not been staying there as a regular inmate?"

"No. She first went to live in a garrison-town t'other side o' Wessex, and since then she's been picking up a living at being a seamstress in Melchester for several months. She only appeared at the Union House on Sunday morning. 'Tis supposed that she walked all the way from Melchester. Why she left her place, I can't say."

Bathsheba's face turned a ghostly white. "Did she walk along our turnpike-road?" she said.

"I believe she did. . . . Ma'am, shall I call Liddy? You don't look well, Ma'am. You look like a lily—so pale and fainty!"

"No. Don't call her. It is nothing. When did she pass Weatherbury?"

"Last Saturday night."

"That will do, Joseph. Now you may go."

"Certainly, Ma'am."

"Joseph, come here a moment. What was the color of Fanny Robin's hair?"

"Really, mistress, I don't really know."

"Never mind. Go on and do what I told you."

She turned away and went indoors, feeling quite faint. About an hour later, she heard the noise of the wagon. Joseph, dressed in his best suit of clothes, was driving. The shrubs and flowers were all piled in the wagon, as she had directed.

Bathsheba, still unhappy, went indoors again. In the course of the afternoon she said to Liddy, who had been informed of the occurrence, "What was the color of poor Fanny Robin's hair?"

"It was light, Ma'am. Real golden hair."

"Her young man was a soldier, was he not?"

"Yes. In the same regiment as Mr. Troy. Troy says he knew him very well."

"How came he to say that?"

"One day I asked him if he knew Fanny's young man. He said, 'Oh yes,' he knew the young man as well as he knew himself, and that there wasn't a man in the regiment he liked better."

"Ah! Said that, did he?"

"Yes. And he said there was a strong likeness between himself and the other young man, so that sometimes people mistook them—"

"Liddy, for Heaven's sake stop your talking!" said Bathsheba, and she ran out of the room.

CHAPTER 42

That afternoon, Poorgrass led the wagon up to the poorhouse. Two men placed a plain pine coffin on the wagon. One of the men stepped up beside it, took from his pocket a lump of chalk, and scrawled upon the cover Fanny's name and a few other words. He covered the coffin with a threadbare black cloth. Joseph then placed the flowers and greens over the coffin as instructed and headed back to Weatherbury.

The afternoon drew on as Poorgrass sat atop the wagon. He felt anything but cheerful, and wished he had the company even of a child or dog. Stopping the horse, he listened. Not a footstep or wheel was audible anywhere around.

At the roadside hamlet called Roy-Town was the old inn—Buck's Head. It was about a mile and a half from Weatherbury. At an earlier time it had been the place where many coaches kept their horses. The stables were now pulled down, and little remained besides the inn itself.

It was a relief to Joseph's heart when the friendly inn came into view. Stopping his horse immediately before it, he entered the inn for a mug of ale.

He was cheered by the sight of Mr. Jan Coggan and Mr. Mark Clark. These were the owners of the two most appreciative throats in the neighborhood.

"Why, 'tis neighbor Poorgrass!" said Mark Clark. "See how pale your face is, Joseph."

"I've had a very pale companion for the last four miles," said Joseph. "And to speak the truth, 'twas beginning to tell upon me. I assure ye, I ha'n't seed victuals or drink since breakfast time this morning."

"Then drink, Joseph, and don't restrain yourself!" said Coggan, handing him a mug three-quarters full.

Joseph drank, and then he drank some more, joined by his two companions. The minutes glided by uncounted, until the skies began perceptibly to deepen. Coggan's pocket watch struck six.

At that moment hasty steps were heard in the entry. The door opened to admit the figure of Gabriel Oak, followed by the maid of the inn bearing a candle.

"Upon my soul, I'm ashamed of you. 'Tis disgraceful, Joseph, disgraceful!" said Gabriel, indignantly. "Coggan, you call yourself a man, and don't know better than this."

"Nobody can hurt a dead woman," said Coggan. "All that could be done for her is done—she's beyond us. Why should a man put himself in a tearing hurry for lifeless clay that can neither feel nor see, and don't know what you do with her at all? Drink, shepherd, and be friends, for tomorrow we may be like her."

Oak looked away in disgust. "As for you, Joseph, you are as drunk as you can be."

Gabriel saw that none of the three was in a fit state to take charge of the wagon for the remainder of the journey. He closed the door upon them and went across to the vehicle. He readjusted the boughs over the coffin and drove the wagon to Weatherbury.

The rumor had gradually spread in the village that the body to be brought and buried that day was all that was left of Fanny Robin. It was also said that she had followed the Eleventh Regiment from Casterbridge through Melchester and onwards. But it had never been revealed that the lover she had followed was Troy. Gabriel hoped that this fact might not come to light for several days. By then the interposing barriers of earth and time would deaden the sting that revelation would have for Bathsheba.

By the time that Gabriel reached her residence, which lay in his way to the church, it was quite dark. A man came from the gate and said through the fog, which hung between them like scattered flour, "Is that Poorgrass with the corpse?"

Gabriel recognized the voice as that of the parson.

"The corpse is here, sir," said Gabriel.

"I am afraid it is too late now for the funeral to be performed with proper decency. We'll put it off till tomorrow morning. The body may be brought on to the church, or it may be left here at the farm and fetched by the bearers in the morning."

Gabriel went indoors to inquire his mistress's wishes on the subject. Troy had not yet returned. Bathsheba said she desired that the girl be brought into the house. Gabriel lighted a lantern and fetched three other men to assist him. They placed the coffin on two benches in the middle of a little sitting-room, as Bathsheba directed.

Every one except Gabriel Oak then left the room. He indecisively lingered beside the body. The very worst event that could in any way have occurred in connection with the burial had happened now. Oak feared Bathsheba might never recover, if she found out that Troy and the dead woman before her had been lovers.

Suddenly, in a last attempt to save Bathsheba from any immediate anguish, he looked again, as he had looked before, at the chalk-writing upon the coffin lid. The scrawl said, "FANNY ROBIN AND CHILD." Gabriel took his handkerchief and carefully rubbed out the two latter words, leaving visible the inscription "FANNY ROBIN" only. He then left the room and went out quietly by the front door.

Chapter 43

"**D**o you want me any longer, Ma'am?" inquired Liddy, at a later hour the same evening. Liddy was standing by the door with a candlestick in her hand. Bathsheba sat cheerless and alone in the large parlor beside the first fire of the season.

"No more tonight, Liddy. But wait—Have you heard anything strange said of Fanny?" The words had no sooner escaped her than an expression of unutterable regret crossed her face, and she burst into tears.

"No—not a word!" said Liddy, looking at the weeping woman with astonishment. "What is it makes you cry so, Ma'am? Has anything hurt you?" She came to Bathsheba's side with a facefull of sympathy.

"No, Liddy—I don't want you any more. I can hardly say why I have taken to crying lately. I never used to cry. Goodnight."

Liddy then left the parlor and closed the door.

Bathsheba was lonely and miserable now. And within the last day or two had come disturbing thoughts about her husband's past.

In five or ten minutes there was a tap at the door. Liddy reappeared and said, "Maryann has just heard something very strange, but I know it isn't true."

"What is it?"

"A wicked story is got to Weatherbury within this last hour—that—" Liddy came close to her mistress and whispered the remainder of the sentence slowly into her ear.

Bathsheba trembled from head to foot.

"I don't believe it!" she said, excitedly. "And there's only one name written on the coffin cover."

"Nor I, Ma'am. And a good many others don't."

Bathsheba turned and looked into the fire, that Liddy might not see her face. Finding that her mistress was going to say no more, Liddy glided out, closed the door softly, and went to bed.

Bathsheba suddenly felt a longing to speak to some one stronger than herself. Where could she find such a friend? If she were to go to Oak now and say no more than these few words, "What is the truth of the story?" he would feel bound in honor to tell her. It would be an inexpressible relief. Nothing further would need to be said.

She flung a cloak round her, went to the door and opened it. She walked slowly down the lane till she came opposite to Gabriel's cottage.

Alas for her resolve! She felt she could not do it. Not for worlds now could she give a hint about her misery to him, much less ask him plainly about the cause of Fanny's death. She must suspect, and guess, and worry, and bear it all alone. With a swollen heart, she went again up the lane, and entered her own door.

Bathsheba paused in the hall, looking at the door of the room where Fanny lay. She locked her fingers, threw back her head, and clasped her hot hands to her forehead, saying, with a hysterical sob, "Would to God you would speak and tell me your secret, Fanny! . . . Oh, I hope, hope it is not true that there are two of you! . . . If I could only look at you for one little minute, I should know all!"

A few moments passed, and she added, slowly, "AND I WILL."

Bathsheba went to the storage closet for a screwdriver. In a short while, she found herself in the small room, quivering with emotion. A fevered mist hung before her eyes, and an intense headache throbbed in her brain. She unscrewed the lid of the coffin and gazed within—

"It was best to know the worst, and I know it now!"

Bathsheba's head sank upon her chest. Her tears fell fast beside the unconscious pair in the coffin. Fanny's face was framed by her yellow hair. There was no longer any doubt as to the origin of the curl owned by Troy. In Bathsheba's heated imagination, Fanny's innocent white face seemed triumphantly aware of the pain she was now causing. Her revenge was complete.

A slamming together of the coach-house doors in the yard brought Bathsheba to herself again. An instant later, the front door opened and closed, steps crossed the hall, and her husband appeared at the entrance to the room, looking in upon her.

Troy stared in astonishment at the scene. "What's the matter, in God's name? Who's dead?"

"I cannot say. Let me go out. I want air!" she stammered.

"No. Stay, I insist!" He seized her hand, and the two of them approached the coffin's side.

The candle was standing on a bureau close by them. The light slanted down, illuminating the cold features of both mother and child. Troy looked in and dropped his wife's hand.

"Do you know her?" said Bathsheba.

"I do," said Troy.

"Is it she?"

"It is."

He had originally stood perfectly erect. But now, he sank upon his knees, with a look of remorse and reverence upon his face. Bending over Fanny Robin, he gently kissed her, as one would kiss a sleeping infant to avoid awakening it.

That gesture impelled Bathsheba to fling her arms round Troy's neck, exclaiming wildly from the deepest deep of her heart, "Don't—don't kiss them! Oh, Frank, I can't bear it—I can't! I love you better than she did. Kiss me too, Frank—kiss me! YOU WILL, FRANK, KISS ME TOO!"

There was something so abnormal and startling in the childlike pain and simplicity of this appeal, that Troy, loosening her tightly clasped arms from his neck, looked at her in bewilderment.

"I will not kiss you!" he said, pushing her away.

"Why not?" she asked, her bitter voice being strangely low.

"I have to say that I have been a bad, black-hearted man," he answered.

"And that this woman is your victim. And I not less than she."

"Ah! don't taunt me, Madam. This woman is more to me, dead as she is, than you ever were, or are, or can be. If Satan had not tempted me with that face of yours, I should have married her. I never had another thought till you came in my way." He turned to Fanny then. "But never mind, darling," he said, "in the sight of Heaven, you are my true wife!"

At these words there arose from Bathsheba's lips a long, low cry of despair. Such a wail of anguish had never before been heard within those long-inhabited walls. It signified the end of her union with Troy.

"If she's—that,—what—am I?" she added, sobbing pitifully.

"You are nothing to me—nothing," said Troy, heartlessly. "A ceremony before a priest doesn't make a marriage."

A vehement impulse to flee from him, to run from this place, hide, and escape his words at any price, overcame Bathsheba now. She turned to the door and ran out.

CHAPTER 44

Bathsheba went along the dark road, neither knowing nor caring about the direction of her flight. She eventually came to a thicket overhung by some large oak and beech trees. She could think of nothing better to do than to stay there and hide. She selected a spot sheltered from the damp fog by a reclining tree trunk. There she sat down and gathered some branches around her for warmth. Then she closed her eyes.

Whether she slept or not that night, Bathsheba was not clearly aware. But it was with a fresher and a cooler brain that she awoke. Day was just dawning. Toward the east, the glow from the yet unrisen sun attracted her eyes. She spied a swamp, dotted with fungi. A morning mist hung over it now like a silvery veil. A form appeared on the other side of the swamp, half-hidden by the mist. It came toward Bathsheba. The woman—for it was a woman—appeared to be searching for something. As the woman approached, Bathsheba realized she was staring at Liddy Smallbury.

Bathsheba's heart bounded with gratitude in the thought that she was not altogether deserted. She jumped up and cried out, "Oh, Liddy!"

"Oh, Ma'am! I am so glad I have found you," said the girl, as soon as she saw Bathsheba.

"Liddy, don't question me, mind. Who sent you—anybody?"

"Nobody. I thought, when I found you were not at home, that something dreadful had happened."

"Is he at home?"

"No. He left just before I came out."

"Is Fanny taken away?"

"Not yet. She will be soon—at nine o'clock."

"We won't go home at present, then. Suppose we walk about in this wood?"

Liddy agreed, and they walked together among the trees.

After some time, Liddy said, "You had better come in, Ma'am, and have something to eat. You will die of a chill!"

"I shall not come indoors yet—perhaps never."

"Shall I get you something to eat, and something else to put over your head besides that little shawl?"

"If you will, Liddy."

Liddy vanished, and at the end of twenty minutes returned with a cloak, hat, some slices of bread and butter, a teacup, and some hot tea in a little china jug.

"Is Fanny gone?" said Bathsheba.

"No," said her companion, pouring out the tea.

Bathsheba wrapped herself up and ate and drank sparingly. A spot of color returned to her face. "Now we'll walk about again," she said.

They wandered about the wood for nearly two hours, Bathsheba replying in monosyllables to Liddy's idle chatter. At length Bathsheba said, "I wonder if Fanny is gone by this time?"

"I will go and see."

She came back with the information that the men were just taking away the corpse.

Liddy then ventured to add: "You said when I first found you that you might never go home again—you didn't mean it, Ma'am?"

"No. I've changed my mind. It is only women with no pride who run away from their husbands. There is one position worse than that of being found dead in your husband's house from his ill usage. That is, to be found alive but living someplace else. A runaway wife is a burden to everybody. Liddy, if ever you marry—God forbid that you ever should!— you'll find yourself in a fearful situation. But mind this, don't you flinch. Stand your ground, and be cut to pieces. That's what I'm going to do."

"Oh, mistress, don't talk so!" said Liddy, taking her hand.

In about ten minutes they returned to the house, entering at the rear. Bathsheba glided up the back stairs to a disused attic, and her companion followed.

"Liddy," she said, with a lighter heart, for youth and hope had begun to return. "You are to be my confidante for the present. I shall reside here for a while. Will you get a fire lighted, put down a piece of carpet, and help me to make the place comfortable? Afterward, I want you and Maryann to bring up the bed from the small room, and a table, and some other things. . . . What shall I do to pass the heavy time away?"

"Hemming handkerchiefs is a very good thing," said Liddy.

"Oh no, no! I hate needlework—I always did."

"Knitting?"

"I despise that, too. No, Liddy, I'll read. Bring up some books."

All that day Bathsheba and Liddy remained in the attic. Bathsheba sat at the window till sunset, sometimes attempting to read, at other times watching and listening, but without much interest.

The sun went down almost blood-red that night, and a livid cloud received its rays in the east. Up against this dark background the west front of the church tower rose distinct. The weathervane atop the spire gleamed gold with the sun's rays. At six o'clock, the young men of the village gathered, as was their custom, for a game of "prisoners' base." They continued playing for a quarter of an hour or so, when the game concluded abruptly.

"Why did the base-players finish their game so suddenly?" Bathsheba inquired of Liddy.

"I think 'twas because two men came just then from Casterbridge and began putting up a grand carved tombstone," said Liddy. "The lads went to see whose it was."

"Do you know?" Bathsheba asked.

"I don't," said Liddy.

CHAPTER 45

When Bathsheba left the house the previous
night, Troy's first act was to cover the dead from
sight. This done, he ascended the stairs and waited
miserably for morning.

His thoughts turned to the day Fanny's body was
brought to the manor house. When dawn arrived on
that day, Troy gathered the twenty pounds he had
gotten from Bathsheba and added another seven
pounds ten he had on hand. Then he left the house
to keep his appointment with Fanny Robin.

On reaching Casterbridge, he left the horse
and trap at an inn, and at five minutes before ten
came back to the bridge at the lower end of the
town. There he waited for Fanny. The clocks struck
the hour, and no Fanny appeared. In fact, at that
moment she was being robed in her grave-clothes at
the Union poorhouse.

A quarter, then a half hour passed. This was the
second time she had broken a serious engagement
with him. In anger he vowed it should be the last.
At eleven o'clock, he jumped from his seat and, in a
bitter mood, drove on to Budmouth races.

He reached the racecourse at two o'clock and
remained there or in the town till nine. But Fanny's
image, as it had appeared to him in the somber

195

shadows of that Saturday evening, returned to his mind. He also recalled Bathsheba's reproaches. He vowed he would not bet, and he kept his vow. On leaving the town at nine o'clock in the evening, he had spent only a few shillings.

He trotted slowly homeward. It was then that the thought first struck him that Fanny had been prevented by illness from keeping her promise. He regretted that he had not remained in Casterbridge and made inquiries. Reaching home, he quietly unharnessed the horse and came indoors, as we have seen, to the fearful shock that awaited him.

As soon as it grew light, Troy arose and stalked downstairs. He left the house by the back door. He walked toward the churchyard, where he found a newly dug unoccupied grave—the grave dug the day before for Fanny. Then he hastened on to Casterbridge.

Reaching the town, Troy entered a side street and entered a stonemason's shop. Stones of all sizes and designs were lying about.

"I want a good tombstone," he said to the man who stood in a little office. "I want as good a one as you can give me for twenty-seven pounds." It was all the money he possessed.

"That sum to include everything?"

"Everything. And I want it now, at once."

"We could not get anything special worked this week."

"I must have it now."

"If you would like one of these in stock, it could be ready immediately."

"Very well," said Troy, impatiently. "Let's see what you have."

"The best I have in stock is this one," said the stone-cutter, going into a shed. "Here's a marble headstone beautifully carved. Here's the footstone carved with the same pattern. And here's the coffin to enclose the grave."

"Get it done today, and I'll pay the money now."

The man agreed. Troy then wrote the words which were to form the inscription, settled the account, and went away.

It was quite dark when Troy left Casterbridge. He carried a heavy basket upon his arm. Troy entered Weatherbury churchyard about ten o'clock and went immediately to Fanny's vacant grave.

Here now stood the tombstone, snow-white and shapely in the gloom.

Troy deposited his basket beside the tombstone and vanished for a few minutes. When he returned he carried a spade and a lantern, the light of which he directed for a few moments upon the marble, whilst he read the inscription. He took from his basket flower-roots of several varieties. There were bundles of snowdrop, hyacinth and crocus bulbs, violets and double daisies, which were to bloom in early spring. Carnations, pinks, lilies of the valley, forget-me-nots, summer's farewell, meadow-saffron and others would flower in later seasons of the year.

Troy laid these out upon the grass and set to work to plant them. He felt a large drop of rain upon the back of his hand. This was followed by a steady rain shower. Troy was weary. It was now almost midnight, and the rain was threatening to increase; he resolved to finish next morning. He entered the church, found a bench, and fell asleep

CHAPTER 46

The tower of Weatherbury Church was erected in the fourteenth century. At the top, elaborately carved gargoyles spouted water from the lead roof of the tower.

While Troy slept in the church, the rain increased outside. Presently, water began to flow off the roof and through the gargoyles down to the ground seventy feet below. One of the gargoyles pointed in the direction of Fanny's grave. As the rain grew more torrential, the water from this gargoyle formed a stream. As the night and the rain wore on, this stream thickened in substance and increased in power.

The torrent from the gargoyle's jaws directed all its vengeance into the grave. The rich earth was stirred into motion, and boiled like chocolate. The flowers so carefully planted by Fanny's repentant lover began to move and writhe in their bed. The winter-violets turned slowly upside down, and became a mere mat of mud. Soon the snowdrop and other bulbs danced in the boiling mass like ingredients in a boiling stew.

Troy did not awake from his comfortless sleep till it was day. Since he had not been in bed for two nights, his shoulders felt stiff, his feet tender, and his head heavy. He remembered his position, arose, shivered, took the spade, and again went out.

The rain had ceased, and the sun was shining through the green, brown, and yellow leaves, now sparkling and varnished by the raindrops.

He entered the gravel path which would take him to Fanny's grave. At one place in the path he saw a tuft of stringy roots washed white and clean. He picked it up—surely it could not be one of the primroses he had planted? He saw a bulb, another, and another as he advanced. Beyond doubt they were the crocuses. Troy turned the corner and then beheld the wreck the stream had made. Nearly all the flowers were washed clean out of the ground.

Troy's face tensed. He set his teeth closely, and his compressed lips moved as those of one in great pain. This accident was the sharpest sting of all. All of a sudden, Troy hated himself. He stood and meditated—a miserable man. Where should he go?

He slowly withdrew from the grave. He did not attempt to fill up the hole, replace the flowers, or do anything at all. He simply surrendered to fate. Going out of the churchyard silently and unobserved—none of the villagers having yet risen—he passed some fields and departed the village.

Meanwhile, Bathsheba remained a voluntary prisoner in the attic of her house. The door was kept locked, except during the entries and exits of Liddy.

Bathsheba did not sleep very heavily that night. Almost before the first faint sign of dawn appeared, she arose and opened the window to breathe in the new morning air. The panes were now wet with trembling tears left by the night rain. From the trees came the sound of steady dripping upon the drifted leaves under them.

Liddy knocked at eight o'clock, and Bathsheba unlocked the door. "What a heavy rain we've had in the night, Ma'am!" said Liddy.

"Yes, very heavy."

"Did you hear the strange noise from the churchyard?"

"I heard one strange noise. I've been thinking it must have been the water from the tower spouts."

"Well, that's what the shepherd was saying, Ma'am. He's now gone on to see."

"Oh! Gabriel has been here this morning!"

"Only just looked in passing—quite in his old way, which I thought he had left off lately. But the tower spouts used to spatter on the stones, and we are puzzled, for this was like the boiling of a pot."

Not being able to read, think, or work, Bathsheba asked Liddy to stay and share breakfast with her. "Are you going across to the church, Ma'am?" Liddy asked. "I thought you might like to go and see where they have put Fanny. The trees hide the place from your window."

Bathsheba had all sorts of dreads about meeting her husband. "Has Mr. Troy been in tonight?" she said.

"No, Ma'am. I think he's gone to Budmouth."

"What makes you think he has gone there?" she said.

"Laban Tall saw him on the Budmouth road this morning before breakfast."

Learning that Troy was not close by, Bathsheba put on her bonnet and walked toward the church. It was impossible to resist the impulse to look upon a spot which, from nameless feelings, she at the same time dreaded to see.

Bathsheba beheld the hole and the tombstone, its delicately marbled surface splashed and stained just as Troy had seen it and left it two hours earlier. On the other side of the scene stood Gabriel. His eyes, too, were fixed on the tombstone. Bathsheba's eyes followed Oak's, and she read the words inscribed on the tombstone:

ERECTED BY FRANCIS TROY
IN BELOVED MEMORY OF
FANNY ROBIN

Oak looked closely to see how these words affected the woman he continued to love. But such discoveries did not much affect her now. Emotional convulsions seemed to have become common occurrences in her life. Bathsheba wished Oak good morning and asked him to fill in the hole with the spade which was standing by. While Oak was doing so, Bathsheba collected the flowers and began replanting them. She requested Oak to get the churchwardens to turn the leadwork at the mouth of the gargoyle. By this means, the stream would be directed sideways, and a repetition of the accident prevented. Finally, she wiped the mud spots from the tombstone, as if she liked its words, and went again home.

CHAPTER 47

Troy wandered along toward the south. He was determined to seek a home anyplace other than Weatherbury. In his mind, that place was too closely associated with the tediousness of a farmer's life, gloomy images of Fanny, remorse, and dislike of his wife's society. Troy continued to wander with extreme languor and depression. The air was warm and muggy, and the former sergeant was growing tired.

His general feeling of malaise was greatly eased when he walked up a hill and saw stretched before him the broad steely sea. Around to the right he spied the port of Budmouth.

He descended and came to a small basin of sea enclosed by the cliffs. Here he thought he would rest and bathe before going farther. He undressed and plunged in. Inside the cove, the water was smooth as a pond. To get a little of the ocean swell, Troy swam between the two projecting spurs of rock. Unfortunately for Troy, a current unknown to him existed outside. Troy found himself carried to the left and then out to sea.

He now remembered the place and its menacing reputation. Many swimmers had perished here, and Troy began to fear that he might be added to their number. Not a boat of any kind was within sight.

The ocean continued to sweep Troy away from land, and he truly believed this might be his last day on earth. Concentrating on the horizon, he spotted a moving object on the waters. It was a rowboat from a larger ship. Swimming with his right arm, he held up his left to hail the sailors. He splashed vigorously and shouted with all his might. The sailors saw him and rowed toward him with a will. Two of the sailors hauled him in over the stern.

Lending him what little clothing they could spare as protection against the rapidly cooling air, they carried him to their vessel. They agreed to row him to land the next morning.

CHAPTER 48

Bathsheba reacted to her husband's absence with a mixture of surprise, relief, and indifference. Strangely, she felt no anxieties about her future life, since anxiety recognizes a better and a worse alternative. She belonged to Troy, and her position was clearly defined—she was doomed. Sooner or later, her husband would be home again. Perceiving clearly that her mistake had been a fatal one, she accepted her fate and waited coldly for the end.

The first Saturday after Troy's departure, she went to Casterbridge alone. As Bathsheba was passing slowly through the crowd, a man spoke some words to another. Bathsheba's ears were keen as those of any wild animal. She distinctly heard what the speaker said, though her back was toward him.

"I am looking for Mrs. Troy. Is that her there?"

"Yes. That's the young lady, I believe," said the person addressed.

"I have some awkward news to break to her. Her husband is drowned."

Upon hearing these words, Bathsheba gasped, "No, it is not true; it cannot be true!" She then fainted.

But not to the ground. A gloomy man, who had been observing her, stepped quickly to her side and caught her in his arms as she sank down.

"What is it?" said Boldwood, looking up at the bringer of the news.

"Her husband was drowned this week while bathing in Lulwind Cove. A coastguardsman found his clothes and brought them into Budmouth yesterday."

Thereupon a strange fire lighted up Boldwood's eye. His face flushed with the suppressed excitement of an unutterable thought. Boldwood lifted Bathsheba and smoothed down the folds of her dress, as a child might have taken a storm-beaten bird and arranged its ruffled feathers. Boldwood then carried her to the King's Arms Inn. Here he placed her on a sofa in a private room.

Bathsheba opened her eyes. Remembering all that had occurred, she murmured, "I want to go home!"

Boldwood left the room. He stood for a moment in the passage to recover his senses. For those few heavenly, golden moments she had been in his arms. She had been close to his heart. He had been close to hers.

Boldwood sent a woman to look after Bathsheba, while he ordered her horse to be harnessed to the gig.

About half an hour later she took her seat and the reins as usual. The first shades of evening were showing themselves when Bathsheba reached home. Leaving the horse in the hands of the boy, she proceeded at once upstairs. Liddy met her on the landing. The news had preceded Bathsheba to Weatherbury, and Liddy looked inquiringly into her mistress's face. Bathsheba had nothing to say.

She entered her bedroom, sat by the window, and thought and thought till night enveloped her. Somebody came to the door, knocked, and opened it.

"Well, what is it, Liddy?" she said.

"I was thinking you must get something to wear," said Liddy, with hesitation.

"What do you mean?"

"Mourning clothes."

"No, no, no," said Bathsheba, hurriedly.

"Why not, Ma'am?"

"Because he's still alive."

"How do you know that?" said Liddy, amazed.

"I don't know it. But wouldn't they have found him, Liddy? I am perfectly convinced that he is still alive!"

Bathsheba remained firm in this opinion till Monday. But then two circumstances joined to shake it. The first was a short paragraph in the local newspaper, which contained a letter to the editor by a young Mr. Barker, M.D., of Budmouth. He claimed to be an eyewitness of the accident. He was passing over the cliff by the cove just as the sun was setting. At that time, he saw a swimmer carried along in the current outside the mouth of the cove. A hill blocked the doctor's view for several minutes. By the time the doctor had climbed to the top, the swimmer had disappeared.

The other circumstance was the arrival of Troy's clothes, when it became necessary for her to examine and identify them.

A strange thought occurred to her, causing her face to flush. Suppose that Troy had followed Fanny into another world. Had he done this intentionally, yet contrived to make his death appear like an accident?

When alone late that evening beside a small fire, Bathsheba took Troy's watch into her hand. The watch had been restored to her with the rest of the articles belonging to him. She opened the case, as he had opened it before her a week ago. There was the little coil of pale hair, the fuse to this great explosion.

"He was hers and she was his. They should be gone together," she said. "I am nothing to either of them. Why should I keep her hair?" She took it in her hand, and held it over the fire. "No—I'll not burn it—I'll keep it in memory of her, poor thing!" she added, snatching back her hand.

CHAPTER 49

Late autumn passed, and winter arrived. No one had seen Troy. Bathsheba now lived quietly. She kept the farm going and raked in her profits without caring much about them.

One result of her general apathy was the long-delayed installation of Oak as bailiff. This, of course, brought him a substantial increase in wages.

Boldwood lived secluded and inactive. Much of his wheat and all his barley of that season had been spoiled by the rain. The uncharacteristic neglect which had produced this ruin and waste became the subject of whispered talk among all the people round. One evening he sent for Oak and asked him to undertake the superintendence of his farm as well as of Bathsheba's. Oak spoke about this to Bathsheba, who reluctantly agreed. Oak now was in charge of about two thousand acres.

A great hope began to arise in Boldwood, who remained as much in love with Bathsheba as ever. It was that should she be willing at any future time to marry any man at all, he would be that man.

Bathsheba's return from a two months' visit to her old aunt at Norcombe afforded Boldwood an excuse for a visit. She was now in her ninth month of widowhood. Boldwood decided to probe her state of mind regarding him. In the middle of the haymaking, Boldwood contrived to be near Liddy, who was assisting in the fields.

"I am glad to see you out of doors, Lydia," he said pleasantly. "I hope Mrs. Troy is quite well after her long absence."

"She is quite well, sir."

"And cheerful, I suppose."

"Yes, cheerful."

"Mrs. Troy puts much confidence in you, Lydia, and very wisely, perhaps."

"She do, sir. I've been with her all through her troubles, and was with her at the time of Mr. Troy's going and all. And if she were to marry again, I expect I should stay with her."

Boldwood throbbed with excitement at these words, which suggested that his beloved had thought of re-marriage.

"When she talks about the possibility of marrying again, you conclude—"

"She never do talk about it, sir," said Liddy.

"Of course not," he returned hastily, his hope falling again. "Well, perhaps, as she is absolute mistress again now, it is wise of her to resolve never to give up her freedom."

"My mistress did certainly once say that she supposed she might marry again at the end of seven years from last year. By that time, her marriage would be void, in case Mr. Troy should reappear."

"Ah, six years from the present time. Said that she might. She might marry at once, in every reasonable person's opinion."

He went away feeling ashamed of having for this one time in his life done anything which could be called underhanded. But he had, after all, uncovered one fact by way of repayment. In little more than six years from this time, Bathsheba might marry him.

This pleasant notion was now continually in his mind. Six years was a long time, but how much shorter than never, the idea he had for so long been obliged to endure!

Meanwhile, the early and the late summer brought round the week in which Greenhill Fair was held. This fair was frequently attended by the folk of Weatherbury.

Chapter 50

The busiest, merriest, noisiest day of the Greenhill Fair was the day of the sheep fair.

Some shepherds marched their flocks for two or three days, or even a week, to display them for sale. The shepherd of each flock marched behind, a bundle containing his kit for the week strapped upon his shoulders.

The Weatherbury Farms, however, were not far from the fairgrounds. Oak led the combined flocks of Bathsheba and Farmer Boldwood to the sheep grounds, old George the dog, of course, behind them.

In another section of the large fair, a large, new circular tent was being set up. Later in the day, a group of performers was scheduled to perform a favorite play. This theatrical production had the elaborate title of "The Royal Hippodrome Performance of Turpin's Ride to York and the Death of Black Bess."

As soon as the tent was completed, the band began to play lively tunes. An elaborately dressed announcer urged fairgoers to attend the performance. Soon crowds of people could be seen streaming into the tent.

At the rear of the large tent were two small

dressing-tents. One of these, reserved for the male performers, was divided into halves by a cloth. In one of the divisions, sitting on the grass, pulling on a pair of boots, was Sergeant Troy.

How did Troy find himself in such a role? The ship that took him aboard was about to start on a voyage, though somewhat short of hands. Troy decided to join the crew. Before they sailed, a boat was dispatched to pick up his clothes, but they were gone.

Troy eventually worked his passage to the United States. There he made an uncertain living in various towns as Professor of Gymnastics, Sword Exercise, Fencing, and Self-defense. He tired of this work and returned to England at last. However, he hesitated to return to Weatherbury Farm for several reasons. Bathsheba was not a women to be made a fool of, or a woman to suffer in silence. Besides, how could he endure existence with a spirited wife he would have to depend on for food and shelter, since he had no money?

Not long before the Greenhill Fair, Troy fell in with a traveling circus. He had impressed the manager with his riding and military talents. It was thus that Troy found himself at Greenhill Fair with the rest of the company on this day.

As the mild autumn sun sank lower, Bathsheba decided she would like to see the performance before going home. Boldwood saw her hesitating before the tent. He came up to her side.

"I hope the sheep have done well today, Mrs. Troy?" he said, nervously.

"Oh yes, thank you," said Bathsheba. "I was fortunate enough to sell them all."

"And now you are entirely at leisure?"

"Yes."

"Am I right in supposing you would like to see the performance, Mrs. Troy? If you would like to, I'll get a seat for you with pleasure." Perceiving that she hesitated, he added, "I myself shall not stay to see it. I've seen it before."

And so a short time after this, Bathsheba appeared in the tent with Boldwood at her elbow. After escorting her to a "reserved" seat, he withdrew.

It turned out that Bathsheba was the only person sitting in the reserved section. Therefore, she stood out among the spectators. Troy, on peeping from his dressing-tent through a slit, saw his wife in the audience. He started back in utter confusion. Although his disguise effectually concealed his identity, he feared that she would recognize his voice.

She looked so charming and beautiful that his reserve about returning to Weatherbury was beginning to decline. He had not expected her to exercise this power over him in the twinkling of an eye. Should he go on, and care nothing? He could not bring himself to do that. There suddenly arose in him now a sense of shame. His attractive young wife, who already despised him, might despise him more by discovering him in so mean a condition after so long a time.

But Troy was never more clever than when

absolutely at his wit's end. He hastily thrust aside the curtain dividing his own little dressing space from that of the manager and proprietor.

"What a miserable situation!" said Troy.

"How's that?"

"Why, there's a creditor in the tent I don't want to see. He'll discover me and nab me as sure as Satan if I open my mouth. What's to be done?"

"You must appear now, I think."

"I can't."

"But the play must proceed."

"Tell the audience that Turpin—Troy's role—has got a bad cold, and can't speak his part, but that he'll perform it without speaking."

After much objection and hestitation, the manager agreed. "I tell you how we'll manage," he said. "I won't tell 'em anything about your keeping silent. Go onstage and say nothing. Do what you can by strategic winks and nods now and then. They'll never find out that the speeches are omitted."

This seemed possible, for Turpin's speeches were not many or long. The appeal of the play lay entirely in its action. And so the play began. The audience cheered and applauded throughout. No one seemed to realize the absence of Turpin's brief speeches. Needless to say, Troy was relieved when it was over and no one had recognized him.

There was a second performance in the evening, and the tent was lighted up. Troy only slightly modified his silent performance, making a few short speeches. As the performance was ending, he observed a man who eyed him carefully. Troy hastily shifted his position, after having recognized the man as Bathsheba's former bailiff Pennyways.

At first Troy resolved to pay no attention to this incident. It was highly probable that he had been recognized. Yet there was room for doubt. It occurred to him that to befriend Pennyways and offer him some money would be a very wise act. He put on a thick beard borrowed from the acting company and went out in search of the former bailiff.

The largest refreshment booth in the fair was provided by an innkeeper from a neighboring town. Troy stood at the entrance to the booth, where a gypsy woman was frying pancakes over a little fire of sticks and selling them at a penny apiece. He could see nothing of Pennyways, but he soon saw Bathsheba sitting with her back pressed against the canvas. Troy went round the tent into the darkness and listened. He could hear Bathsheba conversing with a man. A warmth overspread his face. Surely she was not so unprincipled as to flirt in a fair! He wondered if, then, she reckoned upon his death as an absolute certainty. To better overhear her words, Troy took a penknife from his pocket and softly made two little cuts crosswise in the cloth. By folding back the cloth a bit, he could see and hear his wife.

Troy took in the scene completely now. She was leaning back, sipping a cup of tea that she held in her hand. The owner of the male voice was Boldwood.

Troy found unexpected chords of feeling stirring again within him. She was desirable as ever, and she was his. He nearly rushed in to claim her. Then he thought how the proud girl would hate him on discovering him to be a lowly strolling player.

"Shall I get you another cup before you start, Ma'am?" said Farmer Boldwood.

"Thank you," said Bathsheba. "But I must be going at once."

Bathsheba took out her purse and was insisting to Boldwood on paying for her tea. At this very moment Pennyways entered the tent. Troy trembled. He was about to leave his peephole, attempt to follow Pennyways, and find out if the ex-bailiff had recognized him. However, Troy felt he must listen to the conversation.

"Excuse me, Ma'am," said Pennyways. "I've some private information for your ear alone."

"I cannot hear it now," she said, coldly. That Bathsheba could not endure this man was evident. In fact, he was continually coming to her with some tale or other, by which he might creep into her favor.

"I'll write it down," said Pennyways, confidently. He stooped over the table, took a piece of paper, and wrote upon it the following words—

"YOUR HUSBAND IS HERE. I'VE SEEN HIM. WHO'S THE FOOL NOW?"

This he folded small and handed toward her. Bathsheba would not even put out her hand to take it. Pennyways, then, with a laugh of triumph, tossed it into her lap and left the tent.

Although Troy had not been able to read the note, he had no doubt that it referred to him. "Curse my luck!" he whispered.

Meanwhile, Boldwood said, taking up the note from her lap, "Don't you wish to read it, Mrs. Troy? If not, I'll destroy it."

"Oh, well," said Bathsheba, carelessly, "perhaps it is unjust not to read it. But I can guess what it is about. He wants me to recommend him. Or, it is to tell me of some little scandal or another connected with my work-people. He's always doing that."

Bathsheba held the note in her right hand. Boldwood handed toward her a plate of cut bread-and-butter. In order to take a slice, she put the note into her left hand, where she was still holding her purse. She then allowed her hand to drop beside her close to the canvas. Troy rapidly and noiselessly slipped his hand under the bottom of the tent-cloth, snatched the note from her fingers, dropped the canvas, and ran away. He smiled at the scream of astonishment which burst from her. His object now was to find Pennyways and prevent a repetition of his exposure.

Not far from the entrance to the tent stood Pennyways. Troy glided up to him, beckoned, and whispered a few words to him. With a mutual nod of agreement, the two men went into the night together.

CHAPTER 51

Following the alarming incident in the tent, Bathsheba resolved to drive home in her wagon. But since she had met Farmer Boldwood accidentally (on her part at least), she found it impossible to refuse his offer to ride on horseback beside her as escort. Boldwood mounted his horse and followed in close attendance behind. Thus they made their way toward Weatherbury.

Boldwood was anxious to sound out Bathsheba on her feelings toward him. Shortly, he found an excuse for advancing from his position in the rear, and rode close by her side. They had gone two or three miles in the moonlight, speaking about the fair, farming, Oak's usefulness to them both, and other small subjects, when Boldwood said suddenly and simply, "Mrs. Troy, will you marry again some day?"

This point-blank query surprised her. After a minute or two had passed, she said, "I have not seriously thought of that."

"I quite understand that. Yet your late husband has been dead nearly one year, and—"

"You forget that his death was never absolutely proved, and may not have taken place. I may not be really a widow."

"Not absolutely proved, perhaps, but proved circumstantially. He was seen swimming, and then he disappeared. No reasonable person has any doubt of his death."

"Though I am fully persuaded that I shall see him no more, I am far from thinking of marriage with another."

"Bathsheba, suppose you had complete proof that you are what, in fact, you are—a widow. Would you repair the old wrong to me by marrying me?"

"I cannot say. I shouldn't yet, at any rate."

"But you might at some future time of your life?"

"Oh yes, I might at some time."

"Well, then, do you know that without further proof of any kind, you may marry again in about six years from the present—subject to nobody's objection or blame?"

"Oh yes," she said, quickly. "I know all that. But don't talk of it—seven or six years—where may we all be by that time?"

"They will soon glide by. If I wait that time, will you marry me?"

"But, Mr. Boldwood—six years—"

"Do you want to be the wife of any other man?"

"No indeed! I don't want to talk about this matter now. Perhaps it is not proper. My husband may be living, as I said."

"Of course, I'll drop the subject if you wish. But surely you can say that you will have me back again should circumstances permit? Oh Bathsheba, promise—it is only a little promise, and it will make up for past wrongs—that if you marry again, you will marry me!"

His tone was so aggressive that she almost feared him at this moment, even while she sympathized. It was a simple physical fear—the weak's fear of the strong. This led her to say, "I will never marry another man while you wish me to be your wife. But to say more—you have taken me so by surprise—"

"Let's agree to this—that in six years' time you will be my wife."

She sighed and then said mournfully, "Oh, what shall I do? I don't love you. I much fear that I never shall love you as much as a woman ought to love a husband. If you, sir, know that, and I can still give you happiness by a mere promise to marry at the end of six years, if my husband should not come back, it is a great honor to me. And if you value such an act of friendship, why I—I will—"

"Promise!"

"—Consider, if I cannot promise soon."

"But soon is perhaps never?"

"Oh no, it is not! I mean soon. Christmas, we'll say."

"Christmas!" He said nothing further till he added, "Well, I'll say no more to you about it till that time."

Bathsheba remained troubled for a long time. She felt as though she had been forced, against her will, into making a promise. As Christmas began to approach, her anxiety and confusion increased.

One day she was led by an accident into a dialogue with Gabriel about her difficulty. They were auditing accounts. Something occurred in the course of their labors which led Oak to say, speaking of Boldwood, "He'll never forget you, Ma'am, never."

Bathsheba then poured forth her anxieties concerning Farmer Boldwood. She told Oak what Boldwood had asked her, and how he was expecting her to agree. "The strongest reason for my agreeing to it," she said sadly, "is this: I believe that I hold that man's future in my hand. If I don't give my word, he'll go out of his mind."

"Really, do ye?" said Gabriel, gravely. "Well, I think this much, Ma'am. His life is a total blank whenever he isn't hoping for 'ee. But I can't suppose—I hope that nothing so dreadful hangs on it as you fancy. His natural manner has always been dark and strange, you know. But since the case is so sad and odd, why don't ye give the conditional promise? I think I would."

"But is it right?"

"The real sin, Ma'am, in my mind, lies in thinking of ever marrying a man you don't love honest and true."

She did not reply at once, and then saying, "Good evening, Mr. Oak," went away.

She had spoken frankly. She had neither asked nor expected any reply from Gabriel more satisfactory than that she had obtained. Yet in the depth of her heart there was, at this moment, a little pang of disappointment. Oak had not once wished her free that he might marry her himself. He had not once said, "I could wait for you as well as he." He might have just hinted about that old love of his, and asked, in a playful off-hand way, if he might speak of it. Oak's utter lack of feeling bothered Bathsheba all the afternoon.

CHAPTER 52

Christmas Eve arrived. The talk of Weatherbury was the grand party Boldwood was to give in the evening. What made the party so unusual was that Boldwood should be the giver, for Boldwood rarely attended parties given by others. And it was clear that Boldwood intended the evening to be a memorable celebration. Workers brought a large bough of mistletoe from the woods and suspended it in the hall. Holly and ivy had followed in armfuls. Roasting and basting operations had begun at six that morning in front of the huge fireplace in the kitchen. In the large long hall, the furniture was cleared out for dancing.

Bathsheba was at this time in her room, dressing for the event. She had called for candles, and Liddy entered and placed one on each side of her mistress's mirror.

"Don't go away, Liddy," said Bathsheba, almost timidly. "I am foolishly agitated. I cannot tell why. I wish I were not obliged to go to this party. I have not spoken to Mr. Boldwood since the autumn, when I promised to see him at Christmas on business. I had no idea there was to be anything of this kind."

"But I would go now," said Liddy, who was going with her.

"Yes, I shall make my appearance, of course," said Bathsheba. "But I am the cause of the party, and that upsets me!—Don't tell anyone, Liddy."

"Oh no, Ma'am. You the cause of it, Ma'am?"

"Yes. I am the reason of the party. If it had not been for me, there would never have been one. I can't explain any more. I wish I had never seen Weatherbury. I have never been free from trouble since I have lived here, and this party is likely to bring me more. Now, fetch my black silk dress, and see how it fits me."

Boldwood was also dressing at this hour. A tailor from Casterbridge was assisting him in trying on a new coat that had just been brought home.

Never had Boldwood been so difficult to please. The tailor walked round and round him, tugged at the waist, pulled the sleeve, and pressed out the collar. In the past, the farmer had called such things childish, but tonight would be something special. Boldwood at last expressed himself nearly satisfied and paid the bill. The tailor left just as Oak came in to report progress for the day.

"Oh, Oak," said Boldwood. "I shall of course see you here tonight. Make yourself merry. I am determined that neither expense nor trouble shall be spared."

"I'll try to be here, sir," said Gabriel, quietly. "I am glad indeed to see such a change in 'ee from what it used to be."

"Yes—I must own it—I am bright tonight. I feel as cheerful as a man can be. Perhaps my day is dawning at last."

"I hope it will be a long and a fair one."

"Thank you—thank you. Oak, my hands are a little shaky. I can't tie this neckerchief properly. Perhaps you will tie it for me."

Boldwood approached Gabriel, and as Oak tied the neckerchief, the farmer went on feverishly—

"Does a woman keep her promise, Gabriel?"

"If it is not inconvenient to her, she may."

"—Or rather an implied promise."

"I won't answer for her implying," said Oak, with faint bitterness.

"Well, does a woman keep a promise, not to marry, but to enter on an engagement to marry at some time? Now you know women better than I—tell me."

"I am afraid you honor my understanding too much. However, she may keep such a promise, if it is made sincerely to repair a wrong."

"It has not gone far yet, but I think it will soon—yes, I know it will," Boldwood said. "I have pressed her upon the subject, and she inclines to think of me as a husband at a future time, and that's enough for me. How can I expect more? She has promised—implied—that she will agree to an engagement tonight. Bathsheba is a woman who keeps her word."

Troy was sitting in a corner of The White Hart tavern at Casterbridge, smoking and drinking a steaming mixture from a glass. A knock was heard at the door, and Pennyways entered.

After some bantering back and forth, Troy asked with some anxiety in his voice, "Do you think there's really anything going on between her and Boldwood? Have you found out whether she has encouraged him?"

"I haen't been able to learn. There's a deal of feeling on his side seemingly, but I don't answer for her. Yesterday I heard that she was goin' to the party at his house tonight. They say that she hasn't so much as spoke to him since they were at Greenhill Fair."

"I must go and discover her affections at once— Oh yes, I see that—I must go. I see that my work is well cut out for me."

"How do I look tonight, Liddy?" said Bathsheba, making a final adjustment to her dress before turning away from the mirror.

"I never saw you look so well."

"Everybody will think that I am setting myself to captivate Mr. Boldwood, I suppose," she murmured. "I dread going, yet I dread the risk of wounding him by staying away."

"Now just suppose Mr. Boldwood should ask you—only just suppose it—to run away with him. What would you do, Ma'am?"

"Liddy—none of that," said Bathsheba, gravely. "Mind, I won't hear joking on any such matter. Do you hear?"

"I beg pardon, Ma'am. I won't speak of it again."

"No marrying for me for many a year, if ever. Now get my cloak, for it is time to go."

"Oak," said Boldwood, "before you go, I want to mention something that has been on my mind lately. I would like to increase your share in the farm. That share is too small, considering how little I attend to business now, and how much time you give to it. My intention is ultimately to retire from the management altogether. Then, if I marry her—and I hope—I feel I shall, why—"

"Pray don't speak of it, sir," said Oak, hastily. "We don't know what may happen. So many upsets may befall 'ee. I would advise you not to be too sure."

Oak then left him.

Boldwood continued awhile in his room alone—ready and dressed to receive his company. His anxiety about his appearance gave way to a deep solemnity. He looked out of the window and watched the twilight deepening to darkness.

Then he went to a locked closet and withdrew a small circular case. He was about to put it into his pocket, when he decided to open the cover and peer inside. It contained a woman's finger-ring, set all the way round with small diamonds. Boldwood gazed upon its many sparkles for several minutes.

The noise of carriage wheels at the front of the house became audible. Boldwood closed the box, placed it in his pocket, and went down to greet his guests.

"How does this cover me?" said Troy to Pennyways. "Nobody would recognize me now, I'm sure."

He was buttoning on a heavy gray overcoat with cape and high collar. These nearly came up to a cap which was pulled down over his ears.

Pennyways deliberately inspected Troy. "You've made up your mind to go, then?" he said.

"Made up my mind? Yes; of course I have."

"'Tis a very strange situation that you have got into, sergeant. If I was you, I'd stay as I am—a single man of the name of Francis. A good wife is good, but the best wife is not as good as no wife at all."

"All nonsense!" said Troy, angrily. "There she is with plenty of money, and a house and farm, and horses, and comfort, and here am I living from hand to mouth—a needy adventurer. Besides, it is no use talking now; I've been seen and recognized. What the deuce put it into my head to run away at all, I can't think! But what man on earth was to know that his wife would be in such a hurry to get rid of his name?"

"Well, sergeant, all I say is this, that if I were you I'd go abroad again. There'll be a racket if you go back just now—in the middle of Boldwood's Christmas!"

"H'm, yes. I expect I shall not be a very welcome guest if he has her there," said the sergeant, with a slight laugh. "Ring for some more brandy, Pennyways. I need something to fortify myself. And a stick—I must have a walking-stick."

After emptying his glass in one long swallow, Troy got up to go. "Half-past six o'clock. I shall not hurry along the road, and shall be there before nine."

CHAPTER 53

Outside the front of Boldwood's house, a group of men stood in the dark, waiting to join the celebrations within.

"He was seen in Casterbridge this afternoon—so the boy said," one of them remarked in a whisper. "And I for one believe it. His body was never found, you know."

"'Tis a strange story," said the next. "You may depend upon't that she knows nothing about it."

"Not a word."

"Perhaps he don't mean that she shall," said another man.

"If he's alive and here in the neighborhood, he means mischief," said the first. "Poor young thing. I do pity her, if 'tis true. He'll drag her to the dogs."

"Oh no; he'll settle down quiet enough," said one who took a more hopeful view of the case.

"What a fool to have had anything to do with the man! She is so self-willed and independent, that one is more likely to say 'it serves her right' than pity her."

"No, no. How could she tell what the man was made of? Hello, who's that?" Some footsteps were heard approaching.

"William Smallbury," said a dim figure coming up and joining them. "Dark as a hedge, tonight, isn't it? Be ye any of Boldwood's workfolk?" He peered into their faces.

"Yes—all o' us."

"Oh, I hear now—that's Sam Samway. Thought I knowed the voice, too. Going in?"

"Presently. But I say, William," Samway whispered, "have ye heard this strange tale?"

"What—that about Sergeant Troy being seen, d'ye mean?" said Smallbury, also lowering his voice.

"Aye: in Casterbridge."

"Yes, I have. Laban Tall mentioned it to me but now—but I don't believe it. Hark, here Laban comes himself, 'a b'lieve." A footstep drew near.

"Laban?"

"Yes, 'tis I," said Tall.

"Have ye heard any more about that?"

"No," said Tall, joining the group. "And I'm inclined to think we'd better keep quiet."

They stood silent for a while. Then the front door opened, and Boldwood emerged. He walked slowly down the path. Boldwood passed by the men without seeing them. He paused, leaned over the gate, and breathed a long breath. They heard low words come from him.

"I hope to God she'll come, or this night will be nothing but misery to me! Oh my darling, my darling, why do you keep me in suspense like this?"

Boldwood remained still and silent for a few

minutes. Then, carriage wheels could be heard coming down the hill. They drew nearer and stopped at the gate. Boldwood hastened back to the door and opened it. The light shone upon Bathsheba coming up the path.

Boldwood stifled his inner agitation and politely welcomed her. Then he escorted her into the house, and the door closed again.

"Gracious heaven, I didn't know it was like that with him!" said one of the men. "I thought that fancy of his was over long ago."

"You don't know much of master, if you thought that," said Samway. "I suppose we had better all go in together."

The men entered the hall. The younger men and girls were just beginning to dance. Bathsheba was uncertain how to behave. She was not much more than a slim young girl herself, yet she was also a widow in mourning. She finally resolved to stay for only an hour and then leave unobserved. She had made up her mind that she could not dance, sing, or take any active part in merrymaking.

Bathsheba passed her alotted hour in chatting and looking on. Then she went to the small parlor to prepare for departure.

Nobody was in the room. She had hardly been there a moment when the master of the house entered. "Mrs. Troy—you are not going?" Boldwood said. "We've hardly begun!"

"If you'll excuse me, I should like to go now." Her manner was uneasy. She remembered her promise and feared what he was about to say.

"I've been trying to get an opportunity to speak to you," said Boldwood. "You know perhaps what I long to say?"

Bathsheba silently looked at the floor.

"You do give it?" he said, eagerly.

"What?" she whispered.

"Why, the promise. I don't want to intrude upon you at all, or to let it become known to anybody. But do give your word! Promise to marry me at the end of five years and three-quarters. You owe it to me!"

"I feel that I do," said Bathsheba, "if you demand it. But I am a changed woman—an unhappy woman. I have no feeling in the matter at all. And I don't know what is right to do in my difficult position. But I give my promise, if I must. I give it as the payment of a debt, conditionally, of course, on my being a widow."

"You'll marry me between five and six years hence?"

"Don't press me too hard. I'll marry nobody else."

"Say the words, dear one, and the subject shall be dismissed. Oh Bathsheba, say them!" he begged in a husky voice. "Promise yourself to me. I deserve it, for I have loved you more than anybody in the world! And if I spoke hastily and heatedly, believe me, dear, I did not mean to distress you. I was in agony, Bathsheba, and I did not know what I said. You wouldn't let a dog suffer what I have suffered, if you but knew it! Be gracious, and give up a little to me, when I would give up my life for you!"

The quivering of her dress showed how agitated she was. At last she burst out crying. "And you'll not—press me—about anything more—if I say in five or six years?" she sobbed, when she had regained the power to speak.

"Yes, then I'll leave it to time."

She waited a moment. "Very well. I'll marry you in six years from this day, if we both live," she said solemnly.

"And you'll take this as a token from me."

Boldwood had come close to her side. Now he clasped one of her hands in both his own.

"What is it? Oh I cannot wear a ring!" she exclaimed, on seeing what he held. "Besides, I wouldn't have a soul think that it's an official engagement, because it's not! Don't insist, Mr. Boldwood—don't!" She tried to pull her hand away, and tears filled her eyes again.

"It is simply a pledge—to confirm our arrangement," he said more quietly, but still holding her hand in his firm grasp. "Come, now!" And Boldwood slipped the ring on her finger.

"I cannot wear it," she said, weeping as if her heart would break. "You frighten me, almost. So wild a scheme! Please let me go home!"

"Only tonight. Wear it just tonight, to please me!"

Bathsheba sat down in a chair and buried her face in her handkerchief. At length she said, in a sort of hopeless whisper, "Very well, then, I will tonight, if you wish it so earnestly. Now let go my hand. I will wear it tonight."

"And it shall be the beginning of a pleasant secret courtship of six years, with a wedding at the end?"

"It must be, I suppose, since you will have it so!" she said, fairly beaten into submission.

Boldwood pressed her hand, and allowed it to drop in her lap. "I am happy now," he said. "God bless you!"

He left the room. Bathsheba hid the effects of the last scene as she best could and came downstairs with her hat and cloak on, ready to go. To get to the door, it was necessary to pass through the hall. Before doing so, she paused on the bottom of the staircase to take a last look at the gathering.

There was no music or dancing in progress just now. At the lower end, which had been arranged for the work-folk specially, a group conversed in whispers and with serious looks. Boldwood was standing by the fireplace. He observed their peculiar manner and inquired, "What is it you are in doubt about, men?" he said.

One of them turned and replied uneasily. "It was something Laban Tall heard about, that's all, sir."

"News? Anybody married or engaged, born or dead?" inquired the farmer, gaily. "Tell it to us, Tall. One would think from your looks and mysterious ways that it was something very dreadful indeed."

"Oh no, sir, nobody is dead," said Tall.

"I wish somebody was," said Samway, in a whisper.

"Do you know what they mean?" the farmer asked Bathsheba, across the room.

"I don't in the least," said Bathsheba.

There was a smart rapping at the door. One of the men opened it instantly and went outside.

"Mrs. Troy is wanted," he said, on returning.

"Quite ready," said Bathsheba. "Though I didn't tell them to send for a carriage."

"It is a stranger, Ma'am," said the man by the door.

"A stranger?" she said.

"Ask him to come in," said Boldwood.

The message was given, and Troy, wrapped up to his eyes in coat and hat, stood in the doorway.

There was an unearthly silence, as everyone gazed at the newcomer. Bathsheba was leaning on the stairs. Her face turned alarmingly pale, as she stared rigidly at their visitor.

Troy advanced into the middle of the room and turned to Bathsheba. The poor girl's wretchedness was complete. She had sunk down on the lowest stair, her eyes fixed vacantly on him, as if wondering whether he was a terrible illusion.

Then Troy spoke. "Bathsheba, I come here for you!"

She made no reply.

"Come home with me, come!"

Bathsheba moved her feet a little, but did not rise. Troy went across to her.

"Come, madam, do you hear what I say?" he said, insistently.

Troy stretched out his hand to pull her toward him. She quickly shrank back. This angered Troy, and he seized her arm and pulled it sharply. Bathsheba gave a quick, low scream.

The scream was followed almost immediately by a deafening explosion. The wall shook, and gray smoke filled the room.

Everyone turned to look at Boldwood. At his back was a gun-rack, as is usual in farmhouses. When Bathsheba had cried out, the veins in Boldwood's face had swollen, and a frenzied look had gleamed in his eye. He had turned quickly, taken one of the guns, and fired it at Troy.

Troy fell. He uttered a long gurgling sound, his body contracted for a moment, and he lay still.

The gun was double-barreled. Boldwood turned the gun upon himself. Just as he pulled the trigger, Samway pushed his arm. The gun exploded a second time, sending its contents into the ceiling.

"Well, it makes no difference!" Boldwood gasped. "There is another way for me to die."

Then he broke from Samway, crossed the room to Bathsheba, and kissed her hand. He put on his hat, opened the door, and went into the darkness.

CHAPTER 54

Boldwood walked at an even, steady pace into Casterbridge. He stopped only when he reached the jail, where he summoned the keeper of the prison. After a few words were exchanged, Boldwood entered, and the iron doors closed firmly behind him.

News of the shooting quickly spread throughout Weatherbury. Oak was one of the first to hear of the deed. When he entered the room, the scene was terrible. All the women were huddled against the walls like sheep in a storm. The men were uncertain what to do. Bathsheba was sitting on the floor beside the body of Troy. His head was pillowed in her lap. With one hand, she held her handkerchief to his breast and covered the wound. With the other she tightly clasped one of his. The catastrophe had brought back the decisive Bathsheba of old.

"Gabriel," she said, when he entered, "ride to Casterbridge instantly for a doctor. It is, I believe, useless, but go. Mr. Boldwood has shot my husband."

Oak hurried out of the room, saddled a horse and rode away.

The lateness of the hour and the darkness of the night delayed the arrival of the doctor. He did not arrive for three hours after the shot was fired. When he finally appeared, he learned that Bathsheba had directed that Troy's body be brought to her own house.

The doctor drove at once up the hill to Bathsheba's. The first person he met was Liddy. "What has been done?" he said.

"I don't know, sir," said Liddy, breathing hard. "My mistress has done it all."

"Where is she?"

"Upstairs with him, sir. When he was brought home and taken upstairs, she said she wanted no further help from the men. And then she called me, and made me fill the bath, and after that told me I had better go and lie down because I looked so ill. Then she locked herself into the room alone with him. She would not let a nurse come in, or anybody at all. But I thought I'd wait in the next room in case she should want me. I heard her moving about inside for more than an hour. She said we were to let her know when you or Mr. Thirdly, the local parson, came, sir."

Oak entered with the parson at this moment, and they all went upstairs together. Liddy knocked, and Bathsheba opened the door. She looked calm and nearly rigid.

"All is done, and anybody in the world may see him now," she said. She then walked out of the room.

Looking into the chamber of death, they saw by the light of candles a tall straight shape lying at the further end of the bedroom, wrapped in white. Everything around was quite orderly. The doctor went in, and after a few minutes returned to the landing again, where Oak and the parson still waited.

"It is all done, indeed, as she says," remarked the doctor in a subdued voice. "The body has been undressed and properly laid out in grave clothes. Gracious Heaven—this mere girl! She must have nerves of steel!"

"The heart of a wife merely," floated in a whisper about the ears of the three. Turning, they saw Bathsheba in the midst of them. Then, she silently sank down between them and was a shapeless heap of drapery on the floor.

They took her away into another room. Bathsheba fell into a series of fainting-fits that had a serious aspect for a time. Finally the sufferer was put to bed, and Oak left the house. Liddy kept watch in Bathsheba's chamber. She heard her mistress, moaning in whispers through the dull slow hours of that wretched night: "Oh it is my fault—how can I live! Oh Heaven, how can I live!"

CHAPTER 55

We pass rapidly on into the month of March, to a breezy day without sunshine, frost, or dew. It was the day of Boldwood's trial in Casterbridge.

While the residents of Weatherbury anxiously awaited the verdict, they learned of a discovery made that afternoon. This finding threw more light on Boldwood's conduct and condition than any details which had preceded it.

An extraordinary collection of articles had been found in a locked closet. There were several ladies' dresses, of expensive materials, in Bathsheba's favorite colors. There were two fur muffs. Above all, there was a case of jewelry, containing four heavy gold bracelets and several lockets and rings, all of fine quality. All these things were carefully packed, and each package was labeled "Bathsheba Boldwood." These evidences of a mind crazed with care and love were being discussed in Warren's malt-house when Oak entered from Casterbridge. He came in the afternoon, and his face appeared grave. Boldwood had pleaded guilty and had been sentenced to death.

The discoveries of the closet led several persons to conclude that Boldwood's mind was disturbed.

They recalled that he had been in excited and unusual moods since Greenhill Fair, and he had uncharacteristically neglected his grain stacks the previous summer. A petition was addressed to the Home Secretary requesting a reconsideration of the sentence, based on insanity.

The execution had been fixed for eight o'clock on a Saturday morning about ten days after the sentence was passed. Up to Friday afternoon, no answer to the petition had been received. In Casterbridge, carpenters were lifting a post into a vertical position. Oak had been to town to console Boldwood. It was dark when he reached home, and half the village was out to meet him.

"No news," Gabriel said, wearily. "And I'm afraid there's no hope. I've been with him more than two hours."

"Do ye think he really was out of his mind when he did it?" asked Smallbury.

"I can't honestly say that I do," Oak replied. "However, we can talk about that another time. Has there been any change in mistress this afternoon?"

"None at all."

"Is she downstairs?"

"No. She's very little better now than she was at Christmas. She keeps on asking if you've come, and if there's news. Shall I go and say you've come?"

"No," said Oak. "There's a chance he may still be pardoned. What I've arranged is that Laban Tall shall ride to town later tonight. If there's no news by eleven tonight, they say there's no chance at all."

Laban departed as directed. At eleven o'clock that night, several of the villagers strolled along the road to Casterbridge and awaited his arrival. Among them were Oak and nearly all the rest of Bathsheba's men. At length the tramp of a horse was heard in the distance.

"We shall soon know now, one way or other," said Coggan.

"Is that you, Laban?" said Gabriel.

"Yes. He's not to die. 'Tis imprisonment—for life."

"Hurrah!" said Coggan. And they all joined him in celebrating the news.

CHAPTER 56

Bathsheba revived a little in the spring. However, she chose to remain alone most of the time. She stayed in the house and went no farther than her own garden. She avoided everyone, even Liddy.

As the summer drew on, she spent more of her time outside. One Friday evening in August, she walked to the village for the first time since last Christmas. None of the old color had as yet come to her cheek. As she walked, she heard singing inside the church, and she knew that the singers were practicing. She crossed the road, opened the gate, and entered the graveyard. She came to Fanny Robin's grave and read the inscription. First came the words of Troy himself:

ERECTED BY FRANCIS TROY
IN BELOVED MEMORY OF
FANNY ROBIN,
WHO DIED OCTOBER 9, 18—,
AGED 20 YEARS

Underneath this was now inscribed in new letters:

IN THE SAME GRAVE LIE
THE REMAINS OF THE AFORESAID
FRANCIS TROY,
WHO DIED DECEMBER 24TH, 18—,
AGED 26 YEARS

Bathsheba buried her face in her hands and wept. She did not notice a form that quietly approached her. "Mr. Oak," she exclaimed nervously, "how long have you been here?"

"A few minutes, Ma'am," said Oak, respectfully.

"Are you going in?" said Bathsheba.

"I was," said Gabriel. "I am one of the bass singers, you know. By the way, I wanted to discuss a small matter with you as soon as I could," he said, with hesitation. "Merely about business."

"Oh yes, certainly."

"It is that I may soon have to give up the management of your farm, Mrs. Troy. The fact is, I am thinking of leaving England, maybe next spring."

"Leaving England!" she said, in surprise and genuine disappointment. "Why, Gabriel, why are you going to do that?"

"Well, I've thought it best," Oak stammered out. "California is the spot I've had in my mind to try."

"And what shall I do without you? Oh, Gabriel, I don't think you ought to go away. You've been with me so long—through bright times and dark times—such old friends as we are—that it seems almost unkind."

"Well, good afternoon, Ma'am," he said, in evident anxiety to get away. He left her and went out of the churchyard.

Bathsheba returned home. It pained her that her last old friend was about to leave her.

Three weeks passed. Bathsheba noted that Oak seemed to go out of his way to avoid her. She noticed that Oak entered the small office where the farm accounts were kept only when she was unlikely to be there. Whenever he wanted instructions, he sent a message instead of asking in person. Poor Bathsheba began to suffer now from the most torturing sting of all—a sensation that she was despised.

The autumn wore away, and Christmas Day arrived. Coming out of church that day, Bathsheba looked around, hoping that she might meet Oak. She had heard his bass voice rolling out from the gallery overhead. There he was, as usual, coming down the path behind her. But on seeing Bathsheba turn to look at him, he headed in a different direction.

The next morning, Bathsheba received a letter from Oak. The letter gave official notice that he would not be available for hire come spring.

Bathsheba sat and cried over this letter most bitterly. What should she do now? She hungered for pity and sympathy. In her misery, she put on her bonnet and cloak and went down to Oak's house just after sunset.

A lively firelight shone from the window, but nobody was visible in the room. She knocked nervously, wondering if it were right for a single woman to call upon a bachelor who lived alone. Gabriel opened the door, and the moon shone upon his forehead.

"Mr. Oak," said Bathsheba, faintly.

"Yes, I am Mr. Oak," said Gabriel. "Who have I the honor—Oh, how stupid of me not to realize it was you, Bathsheba! Come in, Ma'am. Oh—and I'll get a light. It is so seldom that I get a lady visitor that I'm afraid I haven't proper furniture. Will you sit down, please? Here's a chair. I am sorry that my chairs have no cushions and are rather hard."

Bathsheba sat down. It was very odd that these two people, who knew each other so well, should feel so awkward and constrained in meeting in a new place. In the fields, or at her house, there had never been any embarrassment.

"You'll think it strange that I have come, but—"

"Oh no; not at all."

"But I thought—Gabriel, I have been uneasy in the belief that I have offended you, and that you are going away on that account. It grieved me very much, and I had to tell you so."

"Offended me! As if you could do that, Bathsheba!"

"Haven't I?" she asked, gladly. "But why else are you going away?"

"I am not going away. I wasn't aware that you wanted me to stay, or I shouldn't ha' thought of leaving," he said, simply. "I have arranged to take possession of Boldwood's farm in the spring. That wouldn't prevent my attending to your business as before, if not for what people have been a-sayin' about us."

"What have people been saying?" said Bathsheba, in surprise.

"The long and short of it is this—that I am grabbing poor Boldwood's farm, with a thought of getting you some day."

"Getting me! What does that mean?"

"Marrying of 'ee, in plain English."

"Marrying me! Such a thing is too absurd—too soon—to think of, by far!"

"Yes, of course, it is too absurd. I don't desire any such thing. I should think that was plain enough by this time. Surely, surely you would be the last person in the world I think of marrying. It is too absurd, as you say."

"'Too—s-s-soon' were the words I used."

"I must beg your pardon for correcting you, but you said 'too absurd,' and so do I."

"I beg your pardon too!" she returned, with tears in her eyes. "'Too soon' was what I said. That's what I meant—too soon—Mr. Oak, and you must believe me!"

Gabriel looked her in the eye. "Bathsheba," he said, tenderly and in surprise, and coming closer, "if I only knew one thing—whether you would allow me to love you and win you, and marry you after all—if I only knew that!"

"But you never will know," she murmured.

"Why?"

"Because you never ask."

"Oh—Oh!" said Gabriel, with a joyful laugh. "My own dear—"

"You ought not to have sent me that harsh letter this morning," she interrupted. "It shows you didn't care a bit about me, and were ready to desert me like all the rest of them! It was very cruel of you, considering I was the first sweetheart that you ever had, and you were the first I ever had!"

"Now, Bathsheba, was ever anybody so provoking," he said, laughing. "You know I was only concerned, from the way people were talking about us, that continuing to work for you might injure your good name. Nobody knows the misery I have been caused by it."

"And was that all?"

"All."

"Oh, how glad I am I came!" she exclaimed, thankfully, as she rose from her seat. "I have thought so much more of you since I fancied you did not want even to see me again. But I must be going now, or I shall be missed. Why Gabriel," she said, with a slight laugh, as they went to the door, "it seems exactly as if I had come courting you—how dreadful!"

"And quite right too," said Oak. "I've danced at your skittish heels, my beautiful Bathsheba, for many a long mile, and many a long day; so I deserve this one visit."

He accompanied her up the hill, and she went happily home. They spoke very little of their mutual feeling. They were such good friends that they did not need pretty phrases. Theirs was the strong feeling which arises when two people first know the worst about each other, and not the best until later on. This is the kind of closeness that usually develops through shared interests and hardships. Unfortunately, it is seldom a part of love between the sexes, because most men and women see each other only in happy times. Where, however, such a relationship exists, it is the only love that is as strong as death. Beside it, the passion usually thought of as love is as fleeting as smoke.

CHAPTER 57

"The most private, secret, plainest wedding that it is possible to have."

Those had been Bathsheba's words to Oak. He now set about to carry out her wishes. The first step was to obtain a license. As he walked into the village for that purpose, he met Coggan. "What's going on tonight, Mr. Oak?" Coggan inquired.

It seemed selfish not to tell Coggan about the impending marriage. Coggan had been true as steel all through the time of Gabriel's unhappiness about Bathsheba. So Gabriel said, "You can keep a secret, Coggan?"

"You know I can."

"Well, then, Bathsheba and I mean to get married tomorrow morning."

"Heaven's high tower! And yet I've thought of such a thing from time to time. I wish 'ee joy o' her."

"Thank you, Coggan. Bathsheba wishes that all the parish shall not be in church for the wedding. She's shy and nervous about it, in fact."

"Ay, I see. Quite right, too, I suppose. And you be now going down to the clerk for the license."

"Yes. You may as well come with me."

After obtaining the necessary legal documents,

they then stopped at the vicar's to arrange for him to perform the ceremony. Then Gabriel went home and prepared for his wedding day.

"Liddy," said Bathsheba, while going to bed that night, "I want you to call me at seven o'clock tomorrow, in case I shouldn't wake."

"But you always wake afore then, Ma'am."

"Yes, but I have something important to do, which I'll tell you about when the time comes. It's best to make sure."

Bathsheba, however, awoke voluntarily at four, nor could she by any means get to sleep again. About six, she could wait no longer. She went and tapped at Liddy's door and awakened her.

"But I thought it was I who had to call you!" said the bewildered Liddy. "And it isn't six yet."

"Indeed it is. Come to my room as soon as you can. I want you to give my hair a good brushing."

When Liddy came to Bathsheba's room, her mistress was already waiting. Liddy could not understand this extraordinary promptness. "Whatever *is* going on, Ma'am?" she said.

"Well, I'll tell you," said Bathsheba, with a mischievous smile in her bright eyes. "Farmer Oak is coming here to dine with me today!"

"Farmer Oak—and nobody else?—you two alone?"

"Yes."

"But is it wise, Ma'am, after what people have been sayin'?" asked her companion, doubtfully. "A woman's good name is such a perishable article that—"

Bathsheba laughed with a flushed cheek, and whispered in Liddy's ear, although there was nobody present. Then Liddy stared and exclaimed, "Souls alive, what news! It makes my heart go quite bumpity-bump!"

"It makes mine rather furious, too," said Bathsheba. "However, there's no getting out of it now!"

It was a damp, disagreeable morning. Nevertheless, at twenty minutes to ten, Oak came out of his house and knocked at Bathsheba's door. Ten minutes later, a large and a smaller umbrella might have been seen proceeding to the church. Oak and Bathsheba were walking arm in arm for the first time in their lives. In the church were Tall, Liddy, and the parson, and in a remarkably short space of time, the deed was done.

The two sat down very quietly to tea in Bathsheba's parlor that evening. It had been arranged that Farmer Oak should go there to live.

Just as Bathsheba was pouring out a cup of tea, their ears were greeted by the firing of a cannon, followed by what seemed like a tremendous blowing of trumpets. "There!" said Oak, laughing, "I knew those fellows were up to something, by the look on their faces."

Oak took up the light and went onto the porch, followed by Bathsheba, with a shawl over her head. The rays of the sun fell upon a group of men gathered upon the gravel in front. When they saw the newly married couple, they all cried, "Hurrah!" At the same moment, the cannon fired again, and the band began to play.

"Those bright boys, Mark Clark and Jan, are at the bottom of all this," said Oak. "Come in, folks, and have something to eat and drink wi' me and my wife."

"Not tonight," said Mr. Clark. "Thank ye all the same, but we'll call at a more seemly time. However, we couldn't think of letting the day pass without a note of admiration of some sort. Here's long life and happiness to neighbor Oak and his lovely bride!"

"Thank ye; thank ye all," said Gabriel.

"Faith," said Coggan, "the man hev learnt to say 'my wife' in a wonderful natural way, considering how very youthful he is in wedlock."

"I never heerd a skillful old married feller say 'my wife' in a more natural way," said Jacob Smallbury.

Then Oak laughed, and Bathsheba smiled, and their friends wished them joy.

Afterword

About the Author

Thomas Hardy never planned to become a writer. His family lived in Dorchester, England, where his father was an accomplished stonemason. Hardy himself was apprenticed to a local architect in 1856, at the age of 16. From 1862 to 1867, he lived in London and showed considerable talent in designing buildings. He won prizes from the Royal Institute of British Architects and the Architectural Association.

Despite his success as an architect, Hardy was drawn to the writing of fiction and poetry. While still employed as an architect, he started to write his first novel, *The Poor Man and the Lady.* Hardy finished this novel in 1867, two years after the end of the American Civil War. However, he could not persuade anyone to publish his work. In disgust, he destroyed the manuscript; only parts of it remain. Hardy then left London and returned to the region of his childhood. There he remained until the end of his life.

Hardy might have given up writing were it not for his mentor and friend, George Meredith. Meredith was a Victorian poet and novelist. He encouraged Hardy to produce another manuscript, which he did. The manuscript was published in 1871 under the title *Desperate Remedies*. His next book, *Under the Greenwood Tree*, was published the following year. In 1873 he published *A Pair of Blue Eyes*, based on Hardy's courtship of Emma Gifford, whom he married in 1874. These three novels were only mildly successful. His next book, however, made him famous. This was *Far from the Madding Crowd*, published in 1874. The book was such a best-seller that Hardy was able to set aside his architectural career and pursue writing full-time.

Far from the Madding Crowd takes place in Wessex, in southwestern England. This became the setting for most of his novels. It is hardly surprising that Hardy should set so much of his writing in rural southwest England. Aside from his stay in London, Hardy spent most of his life there. His detailed descriptions of the countryside and its way of life are among Hardy's most notable achievements. Most of the towns and villages mentioned in his novels do not actually exist, but they are just like the real places that Hardy knew so well.

In the twenty-five years following publication of *Far from the Madding Crowd*, Hardy wrote ten additional novels. These included such classics as *The Return of the Native* (1878), *The Mayor of Casterbridge* (1886), *Tess of the d'Urbervilles* (1891) and *Jude the Obscure* (1895). He also published three short-story collections and more than nine hundred poems.

Unlike *Far from the Madding Crowd*, most of Hardy's novels are filled with pessimism and gloom. Indeed, Hardy himself was a pessimist who believed that dark forces toyed with humans and brought them to grief. Many of his characters are doomed by circumstances beyond their control. Hardy's outlook on life may have been caused by his disbelief in the existence of God. Hardy was an atheist at a time when such disbelievers were universally condemned. Perhaps the undeserved calamities experienced by so many of his characters reflected Hardy's conviction that no higher power would help them in times of trouble. People were on their own against a menacing world.

Hardy's last two important novels, *Tess of the d'Urbervilles* and *Jude the Obscure*, criticized the social order of the Victorian Age. Tess condemns the treatment of women; Jude exposes the pitfalls of marriage. *Jude*, in fact, might have been inspired by Hardy's own personal experience. In the latter years of his marriage to Emma, the two spent much time apart. During these intervals, Hardy formed romantic attachments with other women. *Jude* also blames society for preventing working-class people from obtaining the privileges that upper-class people acquire at birth. Compared to these novels, *Far from the Madding Crowd* seems like a rather innocent—though intensely moving—account of romantic love. In this novel, Hardy makes no attempt to offer a critique of society or to provide a prescription for its betterment. With the possible exception of Fanny Robin, well-meaning characters do not suffer from cruel circumstances beyond their control. In this novel, Hardy is simply telling a story about familiar people, whom he describes in detail. By the end of the novel, we know these people perhaps as well as they know themselves.

After the publication of *Tess of the d'Urbervilles* and *Jude the Obscure*, Victorian readers censured Hardy for his forthright treatment of sex. Some critics even labeled the latter volume "Jude the Obscene." By today's standards, Hardy's handling of sexual matters seems tame indeed. However, in the late nineteenth century, his frankness offended many. Criticism of his writing stung Hardy so deeply that he never wrote another novel after *Jude*. Instead, he turned to poetry, which he continued to publish until his death in 1928 at the age of 87. Had Hardy lived through the Great Depression and World War II, he might well have found affirmation of his gloomy view of life.

The sudden death of Hardy's wife in 1912 also affected him deeply, even though the two had been estranged for a number of years. In 1914 he married his secretary Florence Dugdale, who was 40 years younger than he was.

As is the case with many celebrated figures in English history, Hardy's funeral was held in Westminster Abbey in London. His family and friends wished him to be buried in the family plot at Stinsford. However, his executor insisted that Hardy should be in Poets' Corner in Westminster, where many of England's most renowned writers are buried. The two parties arrived at a compromise. Hardy's heart is buried at Stinsford. His ashes rest in Westminster.

About the Book

Why is *Far from the Madding Crowd*—a novel written well over a hundred years ago—still read today? Surprising as it might seem, this book, published in 1874, was far ahead of its time. It is one of the first novels devoted to the lives of ordinary people in small towns. It features one of the first "liberated women" in literature. Finally, it offers a series of lessons about love and marriage—lessons that many of today's men and women need to learn.

In setting *Far from the Madding Crowd* in a small village in the English countryside, Hardy was doing something quite new. Most literature, particularly up to the nineteenth century, described the lives of kings and queens, princes and princesses, emperors and conquerors. These people, according to the writers, were important and deserved to be read about. However, not every early author agreed. In 1751, the English poet Thomas Gray wrote a poem entitled "Elegy Written in a Country Churchyard." In this poem, Gray celebrated the lives of the ordinary people living in the villages of rural England. According to Gray, we should not make fun of poor people or ignore their stories:

> Let not Ambition mock their useful toil,
>   Their homely joys, and destiny obscure;
> Nor Grandeur hear with a disdainful smile
>   The short and simple annals of the poor.

Later in the poem we find the stanza from which Thomas Hardy chose the title of his novel. Here, Gray praises common people for their hard work and devotion:

Far from the madding crowd's ignoble strife,
  Their sober wishes never learned to stray;
Along the cool sequestered vale of life
  They kept the noiseless tenor of their way.

In writing *Far from the Madding Crowd*, Thomas Hardy brings to life what Gray suggests: he writes about the emotions and behavior of ordinary men and women who lived far away from big cities such as London. Indeed, Hardy convincingly demonstrates that village farmers and tradespeople experience the same feelings and exhibit the same conduct as the worldly citizens of grand cities.

Hardy was well qualified to write about these rural people. He spent much of his own life in the region he calls Wessex, situated in southwestern England. Although Hardy himself was neither a farmer nor a tradesman, he lived among them and knew their ways. For this reason—as well as his writing ability—Hardy paints vivid pictures of planting, harvesting, storing up grain, and the like. He offers believable images of the primitive wagons and other rural conveyances that bumped along the unpaved and rutted roads of the time. Hardy was also familiar with the challenges facing shepherds. He makes us feel we are standing beside Gabriel Oak when he treats the sheep made ill by eating clover.

Scenes of bathing, marking, and shearing sheep come to life in the pages of the novel. Bathsheba's visits to the town fairs, for the purpose of buying and selling, are equally realistic because Hardy himself had seen such events, including amusements like the play in which Troy appears.

Besides writing about everyday people and situations, Hardy also broke with tradition by creating a new sort of female character. In the 1800s, women had few opportunities to earn a living. They could work as servants, nurses, teachers, governesses, and a few other low-paying positions, but they were not expected to take managerial posts. Professions such as banking, business, medicine and the law were reserved strictly for men. No wonder that so many women, denied the options that men possessed, were eager to find husbands! The very fact that Bathsheba was not intent on marrying would have raised eyebrows in the nineteenth century. Her refusal of Oak's and Boldwood's proposals would have seemed strange indeed. After all, weren't women weak, dependent creatures who needed husbands to take care of them financially and protect them from a cruel world?

Imagine, therefore, what the first readers of *Far from the Madding Crowd* must have thought about Bathsheba's behavior after she inherits her uncle's farm. Instead of hiring a bailiff to run the establishment, she decides to manage the farm herself. She calls each worker up to the table and gives him his wages. She walks around her land every evening to make sure that everything is safe.

She even takes it upon herself to go to the town fairs—where she is the only woman present—to buy and sell. The other traders shake their heads and call her "headstrong" for participating in such traditionally masculine activities. Readers of the novel were, no doubt, also shocked by Bathsheba's other "unfeminine" actions. For example, she rides a horse "in an extremely unladylike manner." She literally runs after Farmer Oak to tell him she has no sweetheart. Much later, she takes a horse and carriage and pursues Sergeant Troy to Bath in the middle of the night, intending to end their relationship. By sending Boldwood a valentine, she violates the age-old custom that the man makes the first move in courtship. Even more significantly, she participates in the strenuous daily work of sheep-farming, even risking her life when she climbs the ricks to save her crops from a devastating storm. In creating a character who defies so many social conventions, Hardy reveals that he was a man far ahead of his time.

Finally, *Far from the Madding Crowd* is a surprisingly modern love story. There are three men in Bathsheba Everdene's life: Sergeant Francis Troy, William Boldwood, and Gabriel Oak. Each of these suitors exemplifies a different way of looking at love, and each teaches Bathsheba, and readers today, an important lesson about love and marriage.

Sergeant Troy is exactly the sort of lover many young girls dream of. He is handsome, athletic, and daring. His display of swordsmanship dazzles Bathsheba, as does his appearance in a scarlet tunic with brass buttons. Bathsheba's love for Troy is unthinking, almost instinctive. Her heart shuts out any concerns that he might not be an ideal husband. Once they are married, however, Troy treats Bathsheba badly. He continues to indulge his old wild habits of drinking and gambling. He abandons Bathsheba, disappearing from Weatherbury for more than one year. Worst of all, he breaks Bathsheba's heart when he learns that Fanny Robin has died giving birth to their child. Troy sobs before her coffin, in the presence of Bathsheba, and declares that Fanny is his true wife. At this point, Bathsheba realizes her marriage to Troy is over in all but name. Sadly, her love for Troy was based only on appearance; and, as Bathsheba learns, appearances can be deceiving.

At the opposite extreme is wealthy William Boldwood, twice Bathsheba's age, who falls passionately in love with Bathsheba and proposes marriage both before and after her ill-fated union with Troy. Bathsheba knows she does not care for Boldwood—and even tells him so. A marriage to Boldwood, for her, would be like a business arrangement. Yet she promises to marry him, if Troy does not reappear within six years. This pledge springs not from devotion, but from guilt. Bathsheba feels she owes Boldwood something for having toyed with his affections by sending him an unsigned Valentine's card that said, "Marry me." All she wanted was to make him notice her; she never dreamed he was capable of such an intense emotional response. Bathsheba recoils in horror when Boldwood presents her with a ring to seal their engagement. Despite the protection and financial security Boldwood would provide, despite his own intense devotion to her, Bathsheba knows that a marriage without love would be wrong for her, and Hardy agrees.

If neither a handsome appearance nor a promise of security is a good foundation for marriage, what *should* we look for in a potential mate? *Far from the Madding Crowd* opens and closes with the relationship between Gabriel Oak and Bathsheba. Here we see a different kind of love from those offered by Troy and Boldwood: a steady, mature, lasting love that survives against all odds. Farmer Oak falls in love with Bathsheba practically at first sight and loses no time in proposing marriage to her. Early in the novel, Bathsheba's pride and desire for independence prevent her from accepting Oak romantically. After Oak's sheep are driven over the edge of the cliff, the now-penniless farmer gives up all hope of marrying the woman who has inherited her uncle's grand farmstead. Later, while he is her employee, Oak never ceases to love Bathsheba. However, he suppresses any expression of his feelings due to their different economic stations in life—a situation which, in the 1800s, would have kept them apart.

Although she does not realize it until close to the end of the novel, Oak represents the ideal mate for Bathsheba. He is unerringly honest, reliable and loyal. He knows how to manage a farm and care for its animals. He will look out for Bathsheba's best interests to his dying day. Nevertheless, at the time of their marriage, Bathsheba's devotion to Oak does not measure up to the feverish desire she earlier felt for Troy. And perhaps this is as it should be. In choosing the shallow, selfish Sergeant Troy, young and headstrong Bathsheba follows her heart. In choosing the steadfast and faithful Gabriel Oak, an older, wiser Bathsheba follows her heart as well as her head. Their union will be a true partnership of equals, of friends who share common interests and goals, and who have both had to suffer and learn before being granted happiness.